'You're da  **murmured.**

'If you say so.'

'Yes, I do. Not ⸻ quite captivating with tha⸻

Had she been pouting? Jessica tried to rearrange her features into some semblance of calm. I'm still furious with you, she thought. I still resent it that you feel you can lecture me on my abilities as a mother—even if what you say is true…

But when she looked down, all she could see was the sprinkling of dark hair on his arms. When she breathed, she breathed in the aroma of his maleness. It was powerful, disorientating.

And she knew, before he kissed her, exactly what he was going to do. It was the first time she'd been kissed in years. But she didn't think she'd *ever* been kissed like this before…

Cathy Williams is Trinidadian and was brought up on the twin islands of Trinidad and Tobago. She was awarded a scholarship to study in Britain, and came to Exeter University in 1975 to continue her studies into the great loves of her life: languages and literature. It was there that Cathy met her husband, Richard. Since they married Cathy has lived in England, originally in the Thames Valley but now in the Midlands. Cathy and Richard have three small daughters.

Recent titles by the same author:

THE UNMARRIED
HUSBAND

BY
CATHY WILLIAMS

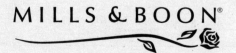

MILLS & BOON®

All the characters in this book have no existence outside the imagination of the author, and have no relation whatsoever to anyone bearing the same name or names. They are not even distantly inspired by any individual known or unknown to the author, and all the incidents are pure invention.

*First published in Great Britain 1998
Harlequin Mills & Boon Limited,
Eton House, 18-24 Paradise Road, Richmond, Surrey TW9 1SR*

© Cathy Williams 1998

ISBN 0 263 80713 4

*Set in Times Roman 10½ on 11¾ pt.
01-9803-50215 C1*

*Printed and bound in Great Britain
by Mackays of Chatham PLC, Chatham*

CHAPTER ONE

THERE was the sound of the front door being opened and shut, very quietly, and Jessica woke with a start. For a few seconds she experienced a feeling of complete disorientation, then everything resettled into its familiar outlines.

She waited, motionless, in her chair, which had been soft enough for her to fall asleep on but too soft to guarantee comfortable slumber, so that now the back of her neck hurt and her legs needed stretching.

She watched as Lucy tiptoed past the doorway, and then she said sharply, 'What time do you call *this*?'

Captured on film, it would have been a comic scenario. The darkness, the stealthy figure creeping towards the stairs, the piercing ring of a voice shocking the figure into total immobility.

Unfortunately, Jessica Hirst didn't find anything at all funny about the situation. She hated having to lie in wait like this, but what else could she do?

'Oh, Mum!' Lucy attempted a placating laugh, which was too nervous to be credible. 'What are you doing up at this hour?'

'It's after two in the morning, Lucy!'

'Is it?'

'It most certainly is.'

'But tomorrow's Saturday! I don't have to get up early for school!'

Lucy switched on the light in the hall, and the dark shape was instantly transformed into a sixteen-year-old teenager. An extremely pretty sixteen-year-old teenager, with waist-length dark hair and hazel eyes. The gauche body of two years ago had mellowed into a figure, so that the woman could easily be discerned behind the fresh-faced child.

Where had the years gone? Jessica straightened in her chair, quite prepared to have this one out here and now, even though she felt shrewish and sleepy, and depressingly like the stereotyped nagging mum.

'Come in here. I want to have a word with you.'

'What, *now*?' But Lucy reluctantly dragged her feet into the sitting room, switching on the overhead light in the process, and slumped defensively into the chair opposite her mother. 'I'm really tired, Mum.'

'Yet not so tired that you couldn't find your way home earlier?' Don't raise your voice, she told herself, try to sound reasonable. Treat her the way you'd treat a possibly unexploded bomb. It seemed odd, though, because she could still remember a squawking, red-faced baby in nappies. And now here she was, sixteen years later, having it out with a rebellious teenager who at times might well have been a stranger. She couldn't quite put her finger on when this transformation had taken place, but certainly in the last few months Lucy had altered almost beyond recognition.

Lucy sighed and threw her a mutinous look. 'I'm not a child, Mum.'

'You are a child!' Jessica said sharply. 'You're sixteen years old…'

'Exactly! And capable of taking care of myself!'

'Do not interrupt me when I'm talking to you!' Which brought another mutinous glare from under well defined dark brows. 'You told me that you would be back by eleven.'

'Eleven! None, but *none* of my friends have to be home by eleven! Anyway, I had every intention of getting back here by then. It's just that…'

'Just that what?'

'You're shouting.'

'I have every reason to shout!' She wanted to march over to the chair and forcibly shake some common sense into her daughter's head. 'Lucy,' she said wearily, 'you're too young to be out and about at these sorts of hours in London.'

'I wasn't "out and about" in London, Mum. You make it sound as though I've been walking the streets! We went to watch a video at Kath's house, and then afterwards…'

'And then afterwards…?' Jessica could feel her stomach going into small, uncomfortable knots. She knew that in a way she was lucky that Lucy would at least still sit and talk to her, where some others might just have stormed off up to bed and locked the door, but that didn't stop her mind playing its frantic games.

She had read enough in the newspapers to be all too aware of the dangers out there. Drugs, drink, Lord only knew what else. Was Lucy sensible enough to turn her back on all of that? She thought so, she really did. But then, at two-thirty in the morning, it was difficult to cling onto reason.

'Well, we went over to Mark Newman's house.' Lucy glanced sheepishly at her mother. 'I wouldn't have gone,' she mumbled, 'but Kath wanted to go, and Mark promised that he'd give me a lift back here. I didn't want to get the underground back.'

As if that made it all right.

'I gave you money for a taxi.'

'I spent it on renting the videos.'

'You spent it on renting the videos.' Jessica sighed, feeling as though she was battling against a brick wall. 'Wasn't that a little short-sighted, Lucy?'

Lucy fidgeted and glared, and then muttered something about her pocket money being inadequate.

'Inadequate for *what*?' Jessica asked tersely, which met with no response this time at all. 'I can't afford to throw money at you, Lucy. I thought you understood that. There's the mortgage to pay off, bills, clothes, food...'

'I know.'

Lucy knew, but Jessica could tell from that tone of voice that knowing and accepting were two different things, and she could feel tears sting the backs of her eyes. Did Lucy imagine that she was economical because she *wanted* to be?

'You could have telephoned me,' she said eventually. 'I would have come to collect you.'

No response. Lately this had been Lucy's way of dealing with all unpleasant discussions between them. She simply switched off.

'So Ruth let Katherine go?' Jessica asked eventually.

'She wasn't there,' Lucy admitted uncomfortably. 'She and Mike have gone to visit some relative or other who's recovering from a stroke.'

'So who was there? Who gave you permission to go to this boy's house? At that hour of the night!'

'Her brother said it'd be all right. I don't know why you're in such a state about this, Mum!'

'Mark Newman... You've mentioned that boy's name in the past. Who is he?' She decided, reluctantly, to let the question of permission from an adult drop. She didn't see that it would get either of them anywhere.

Instead she frowned, concentrating on the familiar

sound of that name, realising with a jolt that it had been on Lucy's lips ever since her daughter had started being more interested in parties than in studying. Who the heck was Mark Newman? No one from her class, certainly. She knew the names of all the children in Lucy's class, and that wasn't one of them.

She swallowed back visions of beards, motorcycles and black leather jackets with names of weird rock groups embroidered on the back.

'Well? Who *is* he, this Mark Newman character?' Jessica repeated sharply. *'Precisely?'*

'No one important,' Lucy said flippantly, eyes diverted, so that Jessica instantly smelled a rat.

'And where does this child live?'

'He's not a child! He's seventeen, actually.'

Oh, God, Jessica thought. An out of work labourer with nothing better to do than prey on young, vulnerable girls like Lucy. Probably a drug pusher. Oh, God, oh, God, oh, God. She could feel her hands, tightly clenched, begin to tremble.

'And what do his parents have to say about this? Turning up at their house with a horde of young girls in tow?' Why am I mentioning parents? she thought. He probably lives in a squat somewhere and hasn't seen his parents in years.

'There's only his dad, and he's never at home. And there weren't hordes of young girls in tow. Just Kath and me.'

'And where, precisely, is home?'

'Holland Park.'

Which silenced some of the suspicions, but only momentarily. Holland Park might not be a squat in the bowels of the East End, but that said nothing.

'Lucy,' she said quietly, 'I know you're growing up,

getting older, but life in the big, bad world can be dangerous.'

'Yes. You've told me that before, Mum.' Lucy looked down, so that her long hair swung around her face like two dark curtains, hiding her expression.

Whoever this Mark Newman was, couldn't he see that she was just a child? Younger than he was, for heaven's sake, and with a fraction of the experience, for all the obligatory black clothes and strange black boots, which Jessica had tried to talk her out of buying!

Her mind accelerated towards thoughts of sex, and skidded to a halt. She just couldn't think of Lucy in terms of having sex with someone.

'Boys, parties…all that can wait, Luce. Right now, you've got your studies. Exams are just around the corner!'

'I know that! As if you ever let me forget!'

'And I don't suppose it's occurred to you that a little study might go a long way towards your passing them?' She could hear her voice raised in alarm at the possibility of her daughter rejecting academic education in favour of education of a different sort. Under the influence of the likes of Mark Newman.

'Can we finish this in the morning? I'm really tired.'

'Do you imagine that you will ever be able to do anything with your life without qualifications?'

'You keep going on about this.'

'Because it's important! Because it's the difference between going somewhere and remaining rooted to…to this…!' She spread her hands expansively, to encompass the small sitting room.

Do you want to end up like me? she wanted to cry out. I made my mistakes, and I've spent a lifetime paying for them.

She didn't want her daughter to go the same way.

But Lucy had switched off. Jessica could see it in the blank expression on her face. The conversation would have to be continued the following day, a semi-permanent onslaught which she hoped would eventually have the effect of water dripping on a stone.

'Go to bed, love,' she said in a tired voice, and Lucy sprang up as though she had been waiting for just such a cue. 'Lucy!'

The slender figure paused in the doorway, looking back over one shoulder.

'I love you, darling. That's the only reason I say these things. Because I care.' She felt choked getting the words out, and once out they barely seemed to skim the depth of emotion she felt towards her daughter.

'I know, Mum.' There was a glimmer of a smile, a bit of the old Luce coming out. 'Love you, too.'

It was after four by the time Jessica was finally in bed, but her thoughts would not let her get to sleep.

Every time she played over these arguments with her daughter in her head she thought back to those days of innocence, when watching Lucy growing up had been like watching a flower unfolding, each stage as fascinating and as beautiful as the one before. First smile, first step, first word, first day at school. Everything so new and uncomplicated.

Just the two of them, locked in a wonderful world. It was easy to forget all the bad times before.

She closed her eyes and realised that it had been a very long time since she had dwelled on the past. It was strange how the years blunted the edges of those disturbing times, until memories of them turned into fleeting snapshots, still sharp but without the power to hurt.

She could have been something. Something more than just a secretary working in a law firm. It didn't matter that they gave her a lot of responsibility, that they entrusted her with a great deal of important work. It didn't even matter that she had picked up enough on the subject to more than hold her own with most of the junior lawyers in the firm.

No. But for circumstances, she could have been one of them. A barrister. Well-read, treading a career path, moving upwards and onwards. Qualified.

Lucy might not appreciate the importance of completing her education, but Jessica was damned if she would let opportunity slip through her daughter's fingers the way that it had slipped through hers.

Mark Newman. The name that had cropped up on several occasions. She racked her brains to try and locate when that name had first been mentioned. Had Lucy mentioned anyone else's?

Jessica couldn't remember, but she didn't think so. No, Lucy had been happily drifting through with her schoolfriends, and her only show of rebellion had been her rapid change of dress code, from jeans and jumpers to long black skirts and flamboyant costume jewellery.

She could remember laughing with Kath's mum at the abrupt transformation, astonished at how quickly it had marked the change from girl to teenager, quietly pleased that really there was nothing for her to worry about.

How on earth could she have been so complacent? Allowed herself to think that difficult teenagers were products of other people? That her own daughter was as safe as houses?

Her last thought as she drifted into sleep was that she would have to do something about the situation. She wasn't going to sit back and let life dictate to her. She would damn well do the dictating herself.

It was only on the Sunday evening, after she had made sure that Lucy sat down with her books, after she had checked her work, knowing that her efforts at supervision were tolerated, but only just, after she had delivered several more mini-lectures on the subject of education—after, in fact, Lucy had retired to bed in a fairly good mood despite everything—that the idea occurred to her.

No point fighting this battle single-handedly.

She could sermonise until she went blue in the face, but the only way she could get Lucy back onto the straight and narrow would be to collect her from school and then physically make sure that she stayed rooted inside the house.

It was an option that she shied away from. Once down that particular road, she might find the seeds she had sown far more dangerous than the ones she was hoping to uproot.

No, there was a better way. She knew relatively little about Mark Newman, but she knew enough to realise that he was an influence over Lucy.

And Mark Newman had a father.

She doubted that she could appeal to the boy's better instincts. A seventeen-year-old who saw nothing wrong in keeping a child of sixteen out until two in the morning probably had no better instincts.

She would go straight to the father.

Naturally, Lucy couldn't be told. Jessica felt somewhat sneaky about this, but in the broader scheme of things, she told herself, it was merely a case of the end justifying the means.

Nevertheless, at nine-thirty, when she picked up the telephone to make the call, the door to the sitting room was shut and she knew that she had the studied casualness of someone doing something underhand.

It hadn't helped that the man was ex-directory and she had had to rifle through Lucy's address book to find the telephone number.

She listened to the steady ringing and managed, successfully, to persuade herself that what she was doing she was doing for her daughter's sake. Most mothers would have done the same.

The voice that eventually answered snapped her to attention, and she straightened in her chair.

'May I speak to Mr Newman, please?'

'I'm afraid he's not here. Who's calling?'

'Can you tell me when he'll be back?'

'May I ask who's calling?'

'An old friend,' Jessica said, thinking on her feet. No point launching into an elaborate explanation of her call. She had no idea whose voice was at the other end of the phone, but it sounded distinctly uninviting. 'I haven't seen Mr Newman for years, and I just happened to be in the country so I thought I'd give him a ring.'

'May I take your name?'

'I'd prefer to surprise him, actually. He and I…well, we once knew each other very well.'

It suddenly occurred to her that there might be a Mrs Newman on the scene, but then she remembered what Lucy had said—'there's only his dad'—and she must be right, because the voice down the line lost some of its rigidity.

'I see. Mr Newman should be back early tomorrow morning. He's flying in from the States and going straight to work.'

Jessica chuckled in a comfortable, knowing way. 'Of course. Well, he hasn't changed!' It was a good gamble, and based entirely on the assumption that men who travelled long haul only to head straight to the office belonged to a certain ilk.

'Perhaps you could tell me where he works? It's been such a while. I'm older now, and the memory's not what it used to be. Is he still…where was it…? No, just on the tip of my tongue…'' She laughed in what she hoped was a genuine and embarrassed manner, feeling horribly phoney.

'City.' The voice sounded quite chummy now. He rattled off the full address which Jessica dutifully copied down and secreted in her handbag.

And tomorrow, Mr Newman, you're in for a surprise visit.

At ten past ten on Sunday evening, sleep came considerably easier.

She made her way to the City offices as early as she could the following morning, after a quick call to Stanford, James and Shepherd, telling them that she needed to have the day off because something unexpected had turned up, and then the usual battle with the underground, packed to the seams because it was rush hour and coincidentally heading into the height of the tourist season.

She had dressed for the weather. A sleeveless pale blue dress, flat sandals. Yet she could still feel the stifling heat seeping into her pores. Temperatures, the weather men had promised, were going to hit the eighties again. Another gorgeous cloud-free day.

She wished that she could close her eyes and forget all these problems. Go back to a time when she'd been able just to whip Lucy along to the park for a picnic, when the nearest thing to defiance had been a refusal to eat a ham sandwich.

She allowed herself to travel down memory lane, and only snapped back to the present, with all its worrying problems, when her destination confronted her—a large office block, all glass and chrome, like a giant greenhouse in the middle of London.

Inside it bore some resemblance to a very expensive hotel foyer. All plants and comfortable sitting areas and a circular reception desk in the middle.

Jessica bypassed that and walked straight to the lifts. She knew what floor the Newman man was located on. She had managed to prise that snippet of information from the unwelcome recipient of her phone call the evening before, still working on the lines of the wonderful surprise she would give him by turning up, and shamelessly using a mixture of charm and flirtatiousness to wheedle the information from him.

The man, she had thought since, would never have made a security guard. Did he dispense floor numbers and work addresses to every caller who happened to telephone out of the blue and claim acquaintanceship with his employer?

But she had been grateful for the information, and she was grateful now as the lift whizzed her up to the eighth floor.

Receptionists, she knew from first-hand experience, could be as suspicious as policemen at the scene of a crime, and as ruthless in dispatching the uninvited as bouncers outside nightclubs. Paragons or dragons, depending on which side of the desk you were standing.

Stepping out on the eighth floor was like stepping into another world.

There was, for starters, almost no noise. Unlike the

offices where she worked, which seemed to operate in a permanent state of seemingly chaotic activity—people hurrying from here to there, telephones ringing, a sense of things that should have been done sooner than yesterday.

The carpet was dull green and luxuriously thick. There was a small, open-plan area just ahead of her, with a few desks, a few disconcertingly green plants, and secretaries all working with their heads down. No idle chatter here, thought Jessica, trying to think what this said about their bosses. Were they ogres? Did they wield such a thick whip that their secretaries were too scared to talk?

She slipped past them, down the corridor, passing offices on her left and pausing fractionally to read the name plates on the doors.

Anthony Newman's office was the very last one along the corridor.

Strangely, she felt not in the least nervous. She had too many vivid pictures in her head of her daughter being led astray by the neglected son of a workaholic for nerves to intrude. If people couldn't rustle up time for their children, then as far as she was concerned they shouldn't have them.

She knocked on the door, not in the least anticipating that the workaholic Newman person might be involved in a meeting somewhere else, and her knock was answered immediately.

Jessica pushed open the door, hardly knowing what to expect, still fuelled by a sense of fully justified parental concern, and was immediately confronted by a large expanse of carpet, an imposing oak desk, and behind that a man whose initial appearance momentarily made her stop in her tracks.

The man was on the phone. His deep voice was barking orders down the line. Not loudly, but with a certain emphatic quietness that made some of her sense of purpose flounder.

She looked at him as he gestured to her to take a seat, and was unwillingly fascinated by the curious, disorientating feeling of power and authority he seemed to give off.

Had she been expecting this? She realised that at the back of her mind she had anticipated someone altogether less forbidding.

It was only when she was seated that she became aware that he was watching her with an equal amount of curiosity. He continued talking, but his cool grey eyes were focused on her, and she abruptly looked away and began inspecting what she could see of his office from where she was sitting.

Not much. Not much, at any rate, that didn't include him in the general picture.

'Who,' he said, replacing the telephone and catching her while her attention was focused on a painting on the wall—an abstract affair whose title she was trying to guess—'the hell are you? What do you want and how were you allowed into my office?'

His voice was icy cold, as was everything about him.

Jessica looked at him and felt a shiver of apprehension which she immediately slapped down.

His was a face, she thought, designed to stop people in their tracks. Everything about it was arresting. It wasn't simply a matter of strikingly well-formed features. More what they revealed. An impression of vast self-assurance and intelligence. He was the sort of man, she thought, who was accustomed to wielding power, to having orders obeyed, to snapping his fingers and having people jump to attention. He was also younger than she had anticipated. Late thirties at the most.

What a shame he obviously couldn't keep a handle on his own son.

Jessica smiled politely, keeping her thoughts to herself.

'I take it you're Anthony Newman?'

'You haven't answered my questions.'

'I'm sorry to barge in on you like this, but I thought that the sooner we had a little chat, the better.'

'If you don't answer me right now,' he said softly, leaning forward, 'then I'm afraid I'm going to have to call a security guard and have you removed from the premises. How did you get in here?'

'I took the lift up and walked down the corridor.'

'I don't have time for games.'

Neither, thought Jessica icily, do you have time for your son. Which is why I'm here in the first place.

'I tried phoning you last night, but I was told that you were away on business and wouldn't be back until this morning.'

'Did Harry tell you where I worked?'

'The man who answered the telephone did, yes.'

He didn't say anything, but there was a look in his eyes that didn't augur well for Harry's fate.

What would he do? Jessica wondered anxiously. Sack the hapless Harry on the spot? Roast him over an open spit? Anything was possible. The Newman man looked like someone who ate raw meat for breakfast.

'You're not going to...do anything...are you?' she asked, worriedly. 'I mean...it wasn't his fault... I implied that you and I were acquaintances...well, quite good friends, actually. I told him that you would be pleasantly surprised to see me...after all this time...

delighted, in fact…' Her voice trailed off, along with a fair amount of her momentum.

'Now, why would you imply anything of the sort?' He looked at her coldly and assessingly, and whereas anyone else might well have been trying to cast their mind back, wondering perhaps whether they knew who she was, she could tell that that wasn't on his mind at all. This man knew quite well that he had never seen her in his life before.

Impressions of him, she realised, were mounting by the second, and none of them were going any distance towards putting her at her ease.

'It seemed the quickest route to getting to see you,' she said flatly, and his eyes narrowed.

'Well, well, well. You don't beat about the bush, do you?'

'I have no reason to.' She didn't care for the look in his eyes, but was damned if she was going to be intimidated. She wasn't easily frightened. Her past had strengthened her, and if he wanted to play mind games with her then he was in for a surprise.

'If you're after money, then I'm afraid you've taken the wrong route.' He glanced down at some documents lying on his desk. Having made his deductions as to her reason for being in his office, his curiosity was giving way to indifference. In a minute, she suspected, he would look at his watch, yawn, then stand up and politely usher her to the door.

'My company already contributes a sizeable amount towards charities.' He linked his fingers together, dragged his eyes away from the document, and looked her over. 'And a little word of advice here—if you want someone to give you a donation, the very last thing you should do is connive your way into their offices and try to catch them off guard. People generally don't care for the element of deviousness involved.'

Jessica found that she was leaning forward in her chair.

'I am not here in connection with a request for money, Mr Newman.'

His eyebrows flew up at that. 'Then why are you here?' Mild curiosity there, she saw. He probably thought that she would get back to the subject of money in a while, after a few byroads to try and divert his attention. A naturally suspicious mind.

'I'm here about your son.'

That worked. It wiped all expression off his face. It was as though shutters had suddenly been pulled down over his eyes.

'And you are…?'

'Jessica Hirst.'

He frowned. 'Well, Mrs Hirst…'

'Miss.'

'Well, *Miss* Hirst, whatever you want to discuss can be discussed on the school premises. If you'd care to see one of my secretaries, she'll fix you an appointment. Frankly, I do think that it's a bit unorthodox to barge your way into my offices.' His frown deepened. 'Why did you involve yourself in a ruse to get this address? Surely it's on the school file?'

'Most probably,' Jessica said calmly. 'But, since I'm not a teacher at your son's school, that wouldn't have done me much good, would it?'

'Then who the heck *are* you?'

Your son is a corrupting influence on my daughter.

Your son is leading my daughter astray.

I'm here to ask you to keep your wretched son away from my daughter.

'My daughter is Lucy Hirst. Perhaps your son Mark has mentioned her to you?'

'What the hell has he gone and done?' His voice was as hard as steel. 'No, Miss Hirst,' he said heavily, 'Mark hasn't said anything to me about your daughter. At least, not that I can recall.' He raked his fingers through his hair and looked at her without flinching.

'Nothing at all?' This time it was her turn to frown, and to wonder whether she hadn't read the signs all the wrong way. Perhaps his name hadn't been dropped into conversations as regularly as she had thought. Maybe she had been mistaken, and the boy was only some kind of acquaintance. Perhaps Lucy's change of attitude had nothing to do with any malign influence at all, and was simply a matter of hormones and puberty kicking in later than she had expected. She had no experience of these things. She could hardly recall her own growing pains, although there had been no room in her disintegrating family life for growing pains to have much space.

'As I said—not that I recall,' he said with a hint of impatience.

'Lucy's mentioned him off and on for months...'

'Well, if you tell me that my son knows your daughter, Miss Hirst, then I'll take your word for it,' he said, by way of response to that remark, and Jessica, who had been lost in her own thoughts, trying to work out whether she had made an utter fool of herself in storming into this man's office full of accusations and demands for a solution, looked fully at him now.

'Are you telling me that you wouldn't know whether your son was seeing my daughter because you don't communicate with him?'

She sounded like a lawyer, she realised. Working

alongside them must have rubbed off on her in more ways than one.

'Listen to me, Miss Hirst, if you think—'

The telephone buzzed, and he picked up the receiver and informed his secretary that no further calls were to be put through.

'Look,' he said, standing up, 'this isn't the right place to have this kind of…conversation. Ellie's not going to be able to keep all my callers at bay.'

He was very tall, and without the desk acting as a shield his presence was even more overwhelming. She discovered that she was watching him, taking in the lean muscularity of his build, the casual air of self-assurance.

'I'll get my chauffeur to take us to the Savoy. We can discuss this there over a cup of coffee and rather more privacy. But I warn you now that my time is limited.'

Jessica nodded. She had planned on taking full control of the proceedings, as she had been taking full control of everything from as far back as she could remember.

Now she felt as though the rug had been pulled from under her feet, but with such dexterity that she was left feeling not unbalanced by the manoeuvre—more disconcerted by the speed.

'Coming?' he asked from the door, and she nodded again and stood up.

CHAPTER TWO

WHAT did he mean that his time was *limited*? Did that imply just right now, or could she read that as a general statement? She should have picked him up on that! Why on earth hadn't she? Didn't he see that this was just the problem? Limited time equalled maladjusted son, who was leading her precious daughter astray!

Jessica felt as though she was losing any advantage she might have had over the proceedings.

Ever since she had stepped into the man's oversized office she had found herself confronted with someone who, even momentarily disconcerted, as he had been, was so accustomed to taking charge of things that he had automatically taken control of the situation. Leaving her utterly lost for words.

And now here she was, with a low table separating them and extravagantly laid out with pots of percolated coffee, cups and saucers and a plateful of extraordinarily mouth-watering little bites.

'So,' he said, crossing his legs and looking at her, 'why have you seen fit to storm into my office and confront me? You might as well tell me right now what my son has been up to. If it's what I think it is, then I'm sure we can settle on some sort of amicable arrangement.'

The wintry grey eyes revealed nothing. There was absolutely nothing about him that encouraged her to relax in any way at all, and she had to resist the impulse not to give in to an embarrassing display of nervous mannerisms. Her self-confidence had ebbed enough as it was, and she was determined that he did not become aware of that.

'Why do you think I came to see you, Mr Newman?' she asked, throwing the question back at him.

'I have neither the time nor the inclination for games, Miss Hirst. I assumed that you were going to tell me precisely that. Wasn't that your reason for barging unannounced into my office?' She stared at him without flinching, and eventually he asked, impatiently, 'Has my son got your daughter into any sort of trouble? Is that it?'

Jessica didn't answer. She decided that the best course of action was to get him to plough his way through this one instead of encouraging her to do all the talking. If a solution was to be engineered, it would have to be a two-way road; he would have to be prepared to travel his fair share of the distance.

'Is she pregnant?' he asked bluntly, and Jessica could feel hot colour rush into her face. The question, with all its implications, was almost an insult.

No, Lucy was not pregnant! She knew that. Why would this man jump to that conclusion? The answer came to her almost as soon as she had asked herself the question—because it was the most obvious cause of concern to a mother. Because boys will be boys. He certainly didn't seem to be shocked by the assumption.

'And what exactly would your solution be if that were the case, Mr Newman?'

'I'm a wealthy man, Miss Hirst. I would be prepared to accept any financial difficulties that might arise.'

'In other words, she would be paid off.'

'Naturally paternity would have to be proved.'

Was this how wealthy people operated? she wondered. Throw enough money at a problem and, hey presto, no more problem? His approach was so cold, so emotionless, that she could feel every muscle in her body tightening in anger.

'That is, if she wanted to keep the baby at all. There are other options, as you well know.'

'Abortion?'

'You make it sound like a crime. But Mark is only seventeen years old, and your daughter… How old is she?'

'Sixteen.'

'Sixteen. Barely out of childhood herself. A baby could well ruin her life.' For the first time he threw her a long, speculative look that took in everything, from the neat little blue dress, well tailored but beginning to show its age, to the blonde bob, to the flat sandals—her only pair of summer shoes, bought in a sale over two years ago. Her wardrobe wasn't bulging at the seams, but everything in it was of good quality, made to last.

The only problem with that was that eventually those made to last items began looking a little stale. Right now she felt downright old-fashioned, and the reason, she knew, lay in those assessing grey eyes.

'You barely look old enough to have a daughter of sixteen.'

'What are you trying to say, Mr Newman?'

'How old were you when you had her?'

'That's none of your business!'

'You expect me to sit back in silence and allow you to lecture me on the behaviour of my son without asking you any questions?' He poured himself a cup of coffee, sat back, and regarded her unsmilingly over the rim of the cup.

Jessica was deeply regretting her impulse to seek this

man's help. He had no intention of co-operating with her and he never would have. He was typical of that breed of person who throws money at their children and assumes that that does the trick. She had seen examples of them often enough where she worked. Parents with too much money and too little time, who sat upright on chairs in the law offices, bewildered by a child who had been brought in for driving a stolen car, or causing damage to property. *How could he do this to us?* was their invariable lament. *After all we did for him!*

'Let's just get one thing straight, Mr Newman.' She refused to call him Anthony. 'My daughter is not pregnant.'

'Then why the hell didn't—?'

'I make that clear from the start?' She looked at the unyielding face. 'Because I was curious to hear precisely how you would have handled such a problem.'

'And I take it from that stony expression on your face that my reply was not what you would have wanted to hear?'

'Very good, Mr Newman.'

'The name is Anthony! Will you stop calling me Mr Newman? I'm not conducting an interview for a job!'

Jessica reddened and looked away.

'And what would have been *your* solution to that particular little problem, Miss Hirst? How would you have suggested that I deal with it?'

'It's irrelevant, since Lucy isn't pregnant.'

'Why don't you answer my question?' He leant forward, resting his elbows on his knees, and subjected her to intense, cool scrutiny. 'I'm interested in your answer.'

'I have no idea.'

'Maybe you would have suggested that I encourage

my son to adopt the mantle of fatherhood at the age of seventeen? Marriage as soon as possible?'

'It's always preferable for a child to have both parents.'

'And does yours? I take it that she doesn't, since you're not a "Mrs".'

'No, there's just me.'

'What happened?' he asked, after a while, and Jessica looked away, feeling cornered but not quite knowing how to extricate herself from the situation.

'There was never a potential husband, if you must know.'

He didn't say anything, and she could well imagine what sort of sordid possibilities were going through his head.

'I'm afraid it just didn't work out quite the way that I'd imagined it.'

'I see.'

'Do you, Mr Newman?'

'Shall I tell you *what* I see, Miss Hirst?' He paused, though not long enough for her to reply, then he leaned forward slightly, and his voice when he spoke was grim. 'I see an anxious young mother who's desperate that her daughter doesn't repeat the same mistakes that she made. That's fair enough, but I really don't think that you've looked at the whole picture, have you? You've somehow got it into your head that my son is to blame for your daughter's behaviour, and I'd be interested in finding out how you arrived at that conclusion.'

The tables had been turned. She had hoped to surprise this man into some sort of favourable response, or at least shared sympathy. But sympathy didn't appear high on his list of virtues, and every word he had just spoken was tantamount to an attack.

'I'm not blaming you in any way,' Jessica informed him, her face burning with anger. She took a deep breath. She was here, he wasn't going to suddenly vanish like a bad dream, and she might just as well make the best of the situation. 'You're right: I'm worried about my daughter and I'm desperate enough to approach someone I've never laid eyes on in my life before.' Fortunately. 'I don't *know* that your son is responsible for Lucy's change of attitude...'

'But you're more than willing to jump to the conclusion...'

'I've put two and two together!'

'And come up with...what...Miss Hirst? Three? Five? Sixteen?'

'Maybe!'' Jessica exploded, keeping her voice down, though she would have loved to yell her head off. 'But then again maybe not! I'm willing to take the chance because I can see my daughter going off the rails bit by bit, and I have no idea how to stop the downward trend!' Her jaw ached from anger and frustration, and a refusal to allow tears to blur the issue.

'Over the past few months she's changed,' Jessica continued in a calmer tone. 'Become difficult. More and more parties, sneaking back into the house at all odd hours. Her schoolwork's taken a back seat. It's only a question of time before her grades start to suffer.' She looked him straight in the eye. 'Lucy doesn't have the advantages of money to tide her through, Mr Newman. She has her brains, but her brains are nothing without her willingness to use them, and right now I'm very much afraid that she might decide not to.'

'What did you have in mind when you came to see me, Miss Hirst?' The coldness had given way to something else, although for the life of her she didn't know what. His expressions, she was fast realising, were difficult to read. He could be thinking anything. But at least he seemed prepared to hear her out.

'I thought perhaps that you could have a word with your son, Mr Newman. I've tried talking to Lucy on numerous occasions, but she switches off.'

'And you think that that would achieve anything?'

'It would achieve more than what's being achieved at the moment, Mr Newman. Right now, I'm more or less living on a battlefield. Occasionally there's a cease-fire, but it never lasts very long, and they seem to be getting increasingly shorter.'

'You still haven't told me why you think my son's responsible. Surely your daughter has lots of friends? How do you know that she isn't being led astray by someone else?'

'I *know* all of my daughter's friends.'

'*All* of them?'

'To the best of my knowledge. I mean, *obviously* I have no definite proof that your son is behind Lucy's change.' In a court of law, she thought, I'd already have lost the case. 'I haven't *overheard* him forcing her to rebel, I haven't found letters from him encouraging sabotage. But his name's been on her lips ever since she started…ever since…this…problem arose.'

'You make my son sound like some sort of subversive force to be reckoned with.' He laughed shortly, as though the notion was utterly ridiculous. As though, she thought suddenly, he was vaguely contemptuous of his son. 'Have you met him?'

'No, but…'

'Then you should reserve judgement until you do, Miss Hirst. What, incidentally, *do* you think is going on?'

'I honestly don't know,' Jessica admitted. 'It's just that your son seems to be very influential over my daughter's life at the moment.'

'Do you think they're sleeping together?' he asked flatly, and she threw him a long, resentful stare.

'It's a possibility, I suppose.' Not one that she was willing to indulge in, but the truth had to be faced.

'Would your daughter tell you if they were?'

'I'm not sure. I'd like to think that she would, but I really just don't know.' It all sounded so vague. Impulse had made her take action, but these questions made her realise that what she felt was so instinctive and nebulous that she could hardly blame him if he refused to co-operate. Aside from which, he was a father, after all, and no one liked the implication that their child was a cor-rupting influence, least of all when the implication came from a perfect stranger.

'Maybe,' she suggested helpfully, 'you could just tell Mark to back away a little, leave her to get on with her life…?'

'He's seventeen years old,' he told her. 'He's hardly likely to relish me telling him what he can and can't do.'

'You're his father!'

'That doesn't necessarily mean that he'll bow his head and listen to a word I say to him,' he informed her tersely. 'You're an intelligent enough woman.' He made it sound as though he had his suspicions about that. 'I'm sure you know precisely what I'm trying to say.'

'That you won't do a damn thing to help. That you'll allow your son to ruin Lucy's life.'

'"Ruin"'s taking it a bit far, isn't it?'

'No, it is not!' This time it was Jessica's turn to sit forward, her hands tightly clenched. She had first-hand experience of what happened when your life suddenly veered off at a tangent and you were left to pick up the pieces. Mark and her daughter might or might not be sleeping together, and if they weren't then she was going to make damn sure that they didn't. Accidents happened, and accidents could change the whole course of your life.

'Look,' she said, in a more controlled voice, 'all I'm asking you to do is have a chat with your son—tell him to wait until Lucy gets a little older if he wants to see her.'

'Maybe send him off to a boarding school somewhere just to make sure?'

'I could do without your sarcasm, Mr Newman.'

'And how do you intend to control your own daughter? How do you know that if Mark obliges and disappears from the scene altogether she isn't going to find another focus of attention?'

It was a sensible enough question, but Jessica still resented him asking it. She stared at him speechlessly, and he looked back without flinching.

'Well?' he asked silkily.

'Of course I don't know!' she exploded furiously. 'But I prefer to cross that bridge when I get to it.'

They both sat back and regarded one another like adversaries sizing up the competition.

'I'll compromise with you,' he said eventually. 'I'll talk to Mark, with you and your daughter present. That way there'll be less of an atmosphere of confrontation and more an air of discussion.'

Jessica stared at him. She hadn't banked on this solution being proffered, and she suspected, judging from the look on his face, that he had only suggested it on the spur of the moment, to get her off his back.

'Would they agree to that?' she asked finally, and he shrugged.

'Possibly not.'

'In which case, at least you can say that you tried…?'

'That's right,' he said with staggering honesty.

'Where do you want this meeting to take place?' Jessica asked, making her mind up on the spot. What he offered was better than nothing.

'I can reserve a private room at a restaurant in Hampstead. Thursday. Eight o'clock. It's called Chez Jacques, and I know the owner.'

'I can't afford that restaurant, Mr Newman.' She voiced the protest without even thinking about it, but she had read reviews of the place and the prices quoted were way out of her reach.

'Fine.' He shrugged and began standing up, and she glared at him.

'All right.'

He sat back down and looked at her.

'But we don't make it an arranged meeting,' she said, deciding that his manipulation had gone far enough. 'I don't want Lucy to think that I've been manoeuvring behind her back…'

'Which you have been…'

She ignored that. 'So we meet by accident. It'll be tricky persuading her to go there, but I'll make damn sure that we turn up.'

'Why should it be tricky? Doesn't she like going to restaurants? Is this part of the teenager phase you say she's going through?'

'Lucy and I don't eat out very often, Mr Newman— Anthony. I take her somewhere on her birthday, and we usually go out on mine, but it's not a habit…'

He frowned, trying to puzzle this one out. 'You surely

can't be that impoverished, if your daughter's at private school…?'

'Private school…? Whatever gave you that impression?'

'Isn't that where she met my son?'

'No, it isn't. I work as a secretary in some law offices. My pay cheque, generous though it is, manages to cover the mortgage and pay the bills and buy the essentials. However, it doesn't quite run to private schooling.'

She hoped that she didn't sound resentful of her state of affairs, or else defensive, but she had a suspicion that that was precisely how she sounded. And she also had a suspicion that that was precisely how he saw her. Wealthy people often led an insular life. They mixed in social circles where foreign travel was taken for granted, as were expensive meals out, best seats at the opera, and cars that were replaced every three years.

Anthony Newman had just been brought face to face with one of those more lowly creatures who didn't lead the charmed life. It wasn't apparent in his expression, but she found herself reading behind the good-looking, detached exterior, even though she was appalled by this inverse snobbery.

She wondered whether he was horrified by the thought of his son mixing with a girl from the wrong side of the tracks. There was nothing in his manner to suggest any such thing, but then he struck her as a man who was clever at concealing what he didn't want the world to see.

He signalled for the cheque, and was irritated when she made an attempt to settle her half of the bill.

'Right. So that's settled then. Eight at Chez Jacques. Thursday.'

'Unless you change your mind and decide to have a quiet word with Mark.'

'Naturally.'

But he had no intention of changing his mind, and when they parted company outside the hotel she wasn't quite sure whether she had done the right thing after all, or not.

She was also taken aback at the reaction he had provoked in her. She had gone to his office to ask for his help, one parent to another. Now she found herself thinking of him, and not simply as a parent. She found herself thinking of him as a man, and a disturbing one at that, although she couldn't put her finger on the reason why. She just knew that his face kept popping up in her head.

For nearly seventeen years she had steered clear of any involvement with the opposite sex. She worked amongst them, went out for drinks occasionally with some of them, in a group, but she was careful never to get involved. Never to get involved was never to be hurt. It was a self-taught lesson. She had her daughter—life would only be complicated if she allowed a man to intrude.

And the decision had hardly cost her dear. In all those years she had never met anyone who had tempted her with the possibility of romance. A few had tried, and she had kindly steered them away. It hadn't been difficult. Most men were frankly unwilling to get involved with a ready-made family unit anyway.

Anthony Newman, however, was in a league of his own. He wasn't like any man she had ever met in her life before. Something about him had aroused a certain curiosity inside her, made her wonder for the first time what she had missed out on during all these years of self-imposed celibacy.

She had to remind herself that curiosity killed the cat.

She was sorely tempted to phone and cancel the dinner arrangement. She knew that he would not have objected. But that, she realised, would have amounted to running away, and it was ridiculous because she didn't even know what she would have been running away from.

He was hardly going to pounce on her, was he? As it was, he had only suggested the arrangement with reluctance, and no doubt he would have been very happy never to clap eyes on her again.

On Thursday morning, just as Lucy was about to head off to school, and Jessica was busy in the kitchen, trying to do twelve things at once before she set out to work, she said, casually, 'By the way, don't arrange anything for this evening. We're going out.'

She could tell from the silence behind her that she might as well have announced that they were departing for a last-minute trip to the moon.

'*Going out? Going out? Going out where?*'

'Going out for a meal, actually.' She turned around, wiped her hands on the kitchen towel, and looked at her daughter. 'People occasionally do things like that.'

'*People* may do things like that, but *we* don't!'

Lucy's eyes were narrowed with suspicion. Her knapsack was half-open and slung over one shoulder, and her long hair was gathered over the other. At sixteen, she was already a couple of inches taller than her mother, and she didn't look like a child. Sixteen. Jessica thought that she looked like an adult of twenty going on thirty something. It was frightening where all the time had gone.

'I thought it might make a nice change,' Jessica said, refusing to be provoked.

'Why?'

Jessica could feel the familiar irritation gathering up inside her, and she swallowed it down and smiled.

'Because it's been a rough few months for us. You've got exams on the horizon. I thought it might be nice to eat out for a change.'

Lucy shrugged and looked suddenly bored with the conversation. 'Okay.'

'So please be home on time!' Jessica told the departing back, a remark which didn't even warrant a response. Lucy was already out of the door and on her way.

By seven-thirty, Jessica was bathed and dressed and waiting in the sitting room for her daughter, who still had not shown up from school. She had taken a magazine to read, so that she could at least pretend to herself that her frame of mind was still relaxed, but the magazine lay unopened on her lap, and her fingers were clasped together.

Now, she thought wearily, there would be another shouting match, and they would arrive at the restaurant with tempers frayed, if they got there at all. Lucy might just not turn up at all.

But turn up she did. Five minutes later. In a rush, and full of apologies.

'Honestly, Mum, I completely forgot. I had to go to the library to check out something for English lit, then I wanted to see Mr Thomas about some maths homework, and by the time I looked at my watch it was after six!' She said this in the voice of someone who was amazed that time could play such a dirty trick on them. 'When do we need to leave?'

'In five minutes. The taxi's booked…'

'Okay.'

Jessica sat back, closed her eyes and felt like someone who had been caught in the path of a wayward tornado. She heard the sound of the shower, rushed footsteps, followed by the slamming of cupboard doors, then Lucy appeared in the doorway dressed in a long black skirt, a pair of ankle boots with laces which had seen better days, and—*where on earth had that T-shirt come from*?

'You can't go dressed like that,' Jessica told her flatly, standing up. 'It's a proper restaurant, Luce, not a burger bar. And that T-shirt is at least ten sizes too small for you. What about that striped cotton shirt I gave you last Christmas? You could tuck it into the skirt and put on some proper sandals.'

'Not again! Stop nagging me!'

'Don't you take that tone of voice with me, my girl!'

'I'm not twelve any longer, Mum!'

'I'm only trying to get you to look a little…'

'More conventional?' She said that as though it were a dirty word.

'If you like, yes. At least tonight.'

'I *like* this outfit. I feel relaxed in it.'

Jessica sighed out of pure exasperation. There was no time left to argue the toss.

'Well, let's just say that I'm not happy with the way you look, Lucy.'

'You're *never* happy with the way I look.'

Here we go again, Jessica thought. Another brief exchange of words developing into an all-out battle. Theoretically, this meal out should have been a relaxed one, but as they were driven to the restaurant she could feel the atmosphere charged with tension. One word on the subject of time-keeping, or dress, or school—or anything, for that matter—and Lucy, she knew, would retreat into moody silence.

'How was school today?' she asked eventually, at which Lucy gave a loud, elaborate sigh.

'You're not going to start going on about homework again, are you, Mum? Not the old boring lecture about the importance of education?'

Jessica felt a prickle of tears behind her eyes.

'I'm just interested, honey.'

'School was as boring as it usually is. Mrs Dean said that it's time we made some decisions about what subjects we want to study in sixth form.'

Jessica held her breath. 'And what have you got in mind?'

'Maths, economics and geography.'

Jessica tried to conceal her sigh of dizzying relief. She had been sharpening her weapons for this battle for quite some time now, making sure that she was well prepared for when Lucy announced that she had decided to quit school at sixteen and get a job in a department store.

'If,' her daughter said casually, 'I bother to do A levels at all. Most of the girls are just going to try and find jobs. Kath's thinking about a computer course. One of those six-month ones. There are always jobs for people who know how to use computers.'

'We've *been* through all this before,' Jessica said, closing her eyes, feeling exhausted. 'You'll get much further in the end if you go on to university, get a degree…'

'While all my friends are out there, earning money…'

'Life isn't just about *tomorrow*, Lucy. You've got to plan a little further ahead than that.'

'Why?'

Jessica gave up. They had been through this argument

so many times recently that it gave her a headache just thinking about it.

The taxi pulled up outside the restaurant, and Lucy said, incredulously, 'We're eating *here*?'

'I thought it might be fun to splash out for a change.' she thought of Mark's father and felt a flutter of nervous apprehension spread through her.

'We can't afford it,' Lucy said, stepping out of the car and eyeing her mother and the restaurant dubiously. 'Can we?'

'Why not?' Jessica grinned. 'You only live once.' And Lucy giggled—an unfamiliar, endearing sound.

Virtually as soon as they walked in Jessica spotted them—seated in silence at a table in the far corner of the room, partially hidden by some kind of exotic plant. She wouldn't have noticed them if she hadn't immediately glanced around the dark, crowded restaurant, looking. Lucy still hadn't seen them. She was wrapped up in excitement at the prospect of eating in a proper restaurant, where waiters hovered in the background and the lighting wasn't utilitarian.

'You should have said that we were coming here, Mum! I would have worn something different.'

'I did mention…'

'Yes, I know!'' Lucy hissed under her breath, as they were shown to their table, her eyes downcast, 'but you *always* tell me that I don't dress properly.'

'You look stunning, whatever you wear,' Jessica murmured truthfully, fighting to keep down the sick feeling in her stomach as they moved closer to where Mark and his father were sitting, still in complete silence. She didn't dare glance at them. She didn't want her eyes to betray any recognition, not even fleetingly. Was he looking at her? she wondered.

She had put a great deal of thought into her outfit. A knee-length dress with a pattern of flowers on it, belted at the waist. It was the sort of dress that could be dressed up or dressed down, and because she had never made the mistake of wearing it to work it still had that special 'going out' feel to it that she liked.

She found herself wondering what sort of image she presented, and was immediately irritated with herself for the passing thought. She frankly didn't give a jot what Anthony Newman thought of her. To him, she was a sudden and inconvenient intrusion. To her, he was merely the means towards an end. It was irrelevant whether he found her attractive or not.

They were about to sit down when Lucy gave a stifled gasp, and Jessica followed the direction of her eyes with what she hoped was polite interest.

'Are you all right?' she asked, playing the part. 'You've gone bright red.'

'Fine. Yes. I'm fine,' Lucy muttered, flustered. She sat down and chewed her lips nervously, darting quick glances at the table behind them. Mature though she looked sometimes, she still had that childish lack of control over the expressions on her face. Jessica could read them like a book. Her daughter had been surprised at the sight of Mark Newman, then deeply embarrassed. Now she was wondering whether she should acknowledge him or not. He still hadn't seen them. His back was to them and his father, after a quick, indifferent glance at them, was now sipping his glass of wine and consulting the menu in front of him.

Jessica pretended to ignore her daughter's agitation. Eventually Lucy said, under her breath, 'I just recognised someone, that's all.'

'Really?' A waiter handed them menus and took an order for aperitifs. 'One of your teachers?'

'No!'

'One of your schoolfriends?' She looked at her daughter over the top of the menu. 'I didn't think that there was anyone here under eighteen apart from you.'

'No one that you know, Mum,' Lucy mumbled, diving into the menu and frowning savagely.

'Oh.'

'He hasn't seen me.'

'*He…?*'

'Don't look around. You'll just make it obvious!'

'Why don't you say hello if you know him, whoever he is?' Jessica asked with studied indifference.

'He's wearing a *jacket*!' She made that sound like a sin, and Jessica did her best not to smile.

'How awful!'

'Very funny, Mum.' She stared at the menu, still red-faced and frowning. 'I suppose I'd better say hi.'

Jessica nodded, holding her breath. 'Good idea, darling.' She placed the menu to one side, having read precisely nothing on it. 'Silly to be antisocial.'

CHAPTER THREE

A FLURRY of introductions. Jessica did her best to appear politely interested, but she was keenly aware of Anthony Newman, the casual, masculine elegance of his body, as he half stood to shake her hand, the feel of his fingers briefly against hers.

'My daughter's mentioned you,' she said, turning to face Mark and scrutinising him for signs of corrupt youth. There were none. He was the unformed younger version of his father. No hard edges yet.

'Is that good or bad?' he asked, grinning awkwardly, and she forced herself to smile back in return.

'Horrendous, I should think,' his father drawled. 'The last thing this child needs is the presence of boys in her life.'

'I'm sixteen,' Lucy said stiffly. 'And I meet boys every day, Mr Newman. My school's co-ed.'

'A mixed blessing, I should think.' Anthony looked at Jessica and she felt herself flush, even though the glance was polite and cursory. 'At least from a parent's point of view.'

'I'm afraid there was no choice...'

'Anyway, why don't you two join us? Unless you're expecting someone else...?'

'We couldn't!' Lucy said quickly.

'We'd love to.' Jessica looked vaguely around her. 'Would they object...?'

'Why on earth should they?' Anthony stood up to pull a chair for her, and at the same time he beckoned to one of the waiters and informed him of the change in seating arrangements.

Even in a matter as small as this there was that authority in his voice that she had noticed a few days ago. A natural air of command which assumed that no arguments would be forthcoming.

Another flurry of sitting down. Poor Lucy looked so dismayed at this change of plan that Jessica almost felt sorry for her.

Was there ever any embarrassment as acute as teenage embarrassment? Jessica looked kindly at her daughter, who was glaring at the empty wineglass in front of her while attempting to mutter a conversation with Mark, and felt suddenly matronly. An ageing, frumpish matron in a flowered dress, gauche in the presence of a man whose interest in her barely rose beyond strictly polite.

She adored Lucy, but where on earth had all that hopeful youth gone?

She felt as though she had been staring at her future one minute, and then the next minute looking over her shoulder at a future long since vanished. In between had been the tricky juggling job of child-rearing and work, hardly time to plan ahead, and no time at all to look behind.

Was that what life was all about? Forgetting what dreams were all about?

She looked under her lashes at Anthony, who was doing his charming best to coax a response out of Lucy, and felt a sudden flare of resentment.

She had been perfectly happy, more or less, until now. For some reason he made her think about her life, and not just her life but the limitations within it. Nothing at all to do with money, more to do with the image she had of herself.

He made her, she realised with annoyance, feel dowdy. Dowdy and mumsy. The sort of woman he might stand and chat to politely at a school gathering, before escaping with a sigh of relief back to his world of glamorous women who had the time and money to pamper themselves.

The conversation had moved on from hobbies—a polite question from Anthony had met with an equally polite answer from Lucy—'None'. Now he was initiating the familiar *school* conversation, and getting, Jessica noticed with amusement, much the same lack of response as when she tried to initiate it herself.

'School's deadly,' Lucy was saying now, tucking into her starter with the enthusiasm of someone who hadn't eaten in several weeks. 'Same old routine every day. I'm surprised some of the teachers don't collapse from the sheer boredom of it all.'

'I remember feeling precisely like that when I was your age,' Anthony said, struggling not to smile. He glanced at Jessica, and they shared a very brief bond of parental understanding.

'Really?' Lucy dragged her attention away from her food for an instant to subject him to a witheringly sceptical stare.

'It gets better in sixth form,' Mark told her.

'If I ever get there,' Lucy muttered under her breath. 'I'm thoroughly fed up with school at the moment. Heaven only knows whether I can face another two years of it.'

'Let's not discuss this here,' Jessica said sharply.

'Why not? Kind of makes a change from discussing it at home all the time. Besides, Mark agrees with me, don't you, Mark? We happen to think that discipline isn't necessarily the best way of learning. Doesn't allow for creativity.'

'That certainly sounds a familiar line of argument.' Anthony shot his son a dark, unreadable stare, and was met with a sullen, unresponsive look in return.

Jessica quietly closed her fork and spoon, and wondered what on earth had possessed her to succumb to this madcap idea of joining forces with Anthony Newman.

As far as good ideas went, it left a lot to be desired. After Anthony's initial lukewarm reception, here they were, seated in one of the more expensive restaurants in London, waging war. They might as well have gone to a fast-food bar—at least the crockery wouldn't have been breakable.

Lucy, having scraped every morsel of food from her plate, was staring at Mark and Anthony with her face cupped in the palm of her hand, seemingly enjoying the terse exchange of words. Lord knows, Jessica thought, what sort of beneficial effect this evening was supposed to be having on her.

'You don't understand, Dad,' Mark was saying in a laboured voice. 'You spend all your life cooped up in an office, and you think that that's the only valid contribution a person can make to society.'

'You're talking absolute rot,' Anthony replied with an edge of anger. 'As usual.'

'Anything you don't agree with, you consider absolute rot.'

Oh, God, Jessica thought, wondering whether she could conceivably excuse herself and spend the next hour in the Ladies. In a minute, they'll be coming to blows.

'We're not here to argue.' Anthony sat back in his

chair, sipped his wine, and smiled cordially at Jessica, who raised her eyebrows in disbelief at this sudden change of attitude. 'Tell me what you do, Jessica.' He linked his fingers together, regarded her with bland interest, and waited.

'Mum works for a bunch of lawyers.'

'I'm sure your mother is capable of answering for herself,' Anthony said.

Mark met Lucy's eyes with sympathy. 'He's always like that. Bossy.' They began chatting in subdued voices while the waiter cleared away the debris, and Jessica smiled rather wildly back at Anthony.

She nervously launched into an explanation of her job, feeling doubly stupid since he already knew what she did for a living.

'She's always wanted to be a lawyer,' Lucy said, interrupting her. 'You know as much as some of the junior ones. You tell me that all the time.'

'Why don't you go back to university and study?' Mark asked with interest. 'There are a lot of mature students around these days.'

Jessica relaxed enough at that to grin. It sounded just the sort of remark that her own daughter would make. 'I'm not sure they'd let me through the doors with my Zimmer frame and dentures,' she said, amused.

'But you could, couldn't you?' Anthony said seriously, focusing on her with curiosity and interest. 'We run courses in my company for anyone interested in studying for professional accountancy qualifications. I'm sure your legal firm would do the same.'

'I'm sure there's no such thing in operation,' Jessica replied, embarrassed at being the sudden centre of interest. 'And I certainly can't take a few years off to go to university. I simply couldn't afford to.'

'Anyway, Mum can't bring heaps of work home. She's much too rushed off her feet coping with me.'

The conversation settled onto a less fraught level. Theatre, cinema, restaurants, travel. Lucy and Mark ate heartily, in relative silence, preoccupied with doing justice to their food, and Anthony chatted pointedly to her, which didn't feel quite right since they were here primarily for another reason. Was he forcing himself to appear polite? It wasn't as though she was his dinner companion for the evening, and it was slightly mortifying to think that he might resent being cooped up here with company he had not particularly wanted in the first place.

It was only when they were sipping their coffee that Jessica felt obliged to have another stab at coming back to what they had arranged this whole unnatural set-up for in the first place.

'And are you,' she asked Mark, virtually apropos nothing, 'going on to university?'

If Lucy realised that he was, then she might stop her vacillating and come to her senses. Peer pressure was a powerful thing, Jessica knew. Mark could probably persuade her to complete her studies far more convincingly than she, her own mother, ever could.

Mark nodded and glanced at his father, who had pushed his cup to one side and was now sitting back in his chair and regarding the proceedings with detached interest.

'That's wonderful!' Jessica said warmly, looking at Lucy and wondering whether she had got the appropriate message. 'Mark's going to university!' she said, just in case.

'I know, Mum. I heard. I *have* got ears, you know.'

'Why don't you ask him what he intends to study?'

Anthony prompted silkily, and Jessica could feel the tension begin to slip back in between them.

'Art.'

'That's great,' she said.

'Why is it great?' Anthony turned to look at her. 'How many jobs can you name offhand that are available for graduates in art?'

This appeared to be a tried and tested point of friction between them. Every family had its own, and right now Jessica did not feel inclined to become embroiled in this one, but she couldn't quite see a way of escape.

'What sort of art?' she asked, and Mark looked at her gratefully.

'Eventually, I'd like to specialise in commercial art. Possibly something to do with computers.'

'Yes, that's all the rage now, isn't it?' she contributed vaguely. 'Computers.'

'That's not what you said when I told you about Kath leaving to do a computer course after exams,' Lucy pointed out with the shrewdness of a barrister in full flow, and Jessica glared at her turncoat daughter.

'I have no objections to computer courses, Luce. I just think that university will suit you better in the long run.'

'Who cares about the long run?' she muttered into her coffee.

'Most prospective employers,' Anthony pointed out. 'Having a degree is a distinct advantage. Especially,' he added coldly, eyeing his son, 'when it's a degree in a sensible subject. What do you intend to study, should you decide to go?'

'Economics.'

'Excellent option.' Anthony shot his son a look that seemed to say, *Hear that?*

'It's the easiest thing I can think of. I'm good at maths and sciences but hopeless at all that arty stuff.'

Jessica was beginning to see Mark's appeal to her daughter. He was creative, artistic—he operated with confidence in a field in which she would always be little more than an onlooker. He was also, Jessica thought with relief, down to earth—not the hell-raiser she had originally imagined.

From that point of view, if nothing else, the arranged dinner had been a success, because it had set her mind at rest. Lucy's behaviour might have changed dramatically over the past few months, but there was no point in trying to pin the blame on any one person. She had changed because she was in the difficult process of growing up, and there was nothing that could be done to ease the transition.

She was vaguely aware of conversation going on around her, then Lucy's voice asking Mark whether he was interested in going to a party. At which, Jessica's head shot up and she said quickly, 'Out of the question.'

'It's not really a party,' Lucy said, mouth downturned. 'Kath and a few of the others are going to a club to hear her brother's band.'

'I'm not interested in where Kath and her friends are going,' Jessica said sharply. '*You're* heading home with me. Tomorrow's school, and…'

'And I have to get an early night. Mum! That's what you used to tell me when I was eight years old! Besides—' she looked at her watch '—it's only just gone nine-thirty.'

Nine-thirty! For Jessica the night was hardly young at nine-thirty. She was usually in bed by ten o'clock, exhausted after a day at work, grateful for sleep.

'That's not the point,' Jessica said, shying away from

informing her daughter in company that nine-thirty was hardly the start of the evening. She could feel Anthony following this little exchange with interest, and she instinctively knew that he certainly would not be a person who found himself tucked into bed by ten most nights. She had a feeling that he would be highly amused by any such admission on her part, and there was no way that she was going to provide a cheap source of amusement for him.

'Well, what is?' Lucy insisted, not backing down. She folded her arms and challenged her mother to prolong the argument.

'The point is…' Jessica began.

'Why don't you let her go?' Anthony said smoothly, to Jessica's fury. 'As a one-off. After all, it's been something of an evening…'

Jessica turned to face him angrily. 'I really don't think that it's any concern of yours, Mr Newman.'

'Oh, come on, Mum. Don't be such a stick-in-the-mud! Anyone would think that you were never young!'

I never *was*, Jessica felt like crying out. I was saddled with responsibility before I even knew what youth felt like. I don't regret any of it, but that's just a fact!

'I'll make sure that she's back home by eleven,' Mark said helpfully. 'This club's only about five minutes from here, and I'll drop her back afterwards.'

'Fine,' Jessica agreed through gritted teeth. Outnumbered, outvoted and outraged. That was precisely how she felt. Lucy was beaming now that she had got her own way, irrespective of the fact that it had hardly been a fair fight. She couldn't wait to be on her way. She began chatting to Mark and there was real animation on her face, none of the stilted politeness that had been there earlier on.

'Why don't you two go?' Anthony suggested. He looked at Lucy. 'I'll drop your mother back home.' Which silenced Lucy. She eyed them quickly, then shrugged and stood up.

As soon as they were on their way out, Jessica turned to Anthony furiously.

'How dare you? How dare you *butt in* and encourage her to go nightclubbing at this hour? You agreed to all this because I needed your *help*!'

'Has it occurred to you that that was exactly what I thought I was giving?'

'No.'

'What was there to gain by putting your foot down? You would probably both have got back home and argued the point until midnight anyway.'

He was so damned calm about the whole thing that Jessica wanted to scream. He linked his fingers together and regarded her unsmilingly.

'My daughter is not your responsibility, Mr Newman. If I decide that we go home and argue until midnight, then that's entirely my decision. It has nothing to do with you!'

'Fair enough.' He shrugged. 'In that case, please accept my apologies.'

Except he wasn't sorry. Not at all. He was merely being diplomatic because that seemed the most trouble-free option. In a very short while he would be in his taxi, or his car, or whatever else he had come in, zooming out of her life and away from her headaches.

'And, if you don't mind, I'll settle my half of the bill,' she informed him coldly. Which she duly did, trying not to gulp at the amount. As a single parent without much money to spare, she had developed over the years the unnerving habit of translating in her mind every little luxury into necessities that could be bought for the same amount.

And paying didn't make her feel much better either. She just felt petulant, like a child trying to make a stand.

'I've got my car,' he said, standing up, and allowing her to precede him to the door. 'I'll give you a lift to your house.'

'I'm fine. I can get a taxi.'

'Oh, for God's sake, don't be so bloody stubborn.' Which made her glower at him. 'Besides, I want to talk to you about this evening.'

Jessica looked at him narrowly, wondering whether she should be suspicious or not. He had risen to the occasion, done his part, engineered the meeting, however useless it might turn out to be—what was there to discuss?

'Where do you live?' he asked, strolling towards his car and opening the passenger door for her.

He got in, started the engine, and turned in his seat to look at her.

How, she wondered, could such an enormous car suddenly seem so tiny?

She could feel his presence pressing down on her, suffocating. When she looked at him, her heart seemed to do a series of uncomfortable little leaps inside her chest, before settling back down. A nerve-racking sensation. Anyone would think that he was the first man she had come into contact with for decades! She forced a nonchalant smile to her face at that inner joke, told him where she lived, and then allowed him the privilege of trying to work out how to get there.

'I usually take the underground,' she said politely, deciding that the safest thing to do as far as her pulse rate went was to avoid looking directly at him. 'I really have no idea of the layout of the roads in London. I mean, I can get to a few tried and tested places, but that's about it, I'm afraid.'

'Very complicated network,' he agreed, pulling away from the kerb with every appearance of knowing where he was going, after briefly consulting an A-Z.

'You don't seem to find it too overwhelming,' Jessica pointed out after a while.

'I used to work as a taxi driver.'

'Not really?'

'You're right. Not really.' He glanced quickly at her and grinned, and she found herself, somehow, smiling back in return. 'So your mood does occasionally lighten!'

'Occasionally,' Jessica admitted. 'Although I give my mind strict instructions not to let that happen too often.'

He laughed at that, and reluctantly she gazed across at him, using the darkness in the car as a shield, to linger on his face, the curve of his mouth, still smiling slightly, the strength of his features.

Physically, she thought, he really was remarkable. Or at any rate mesmerising, though she couldn't put her finger on why.

'Why not?' He shot her a quick glance, then looked back at the road. 'Doesn't your boyfriend approve of a sense of humour?'

'I haven't got a boyfriend,' Jessica told him abruptly. 'Lucy takes up all my time.'

'I see.'

No, you don't, she wanted to inform him. You don't see at all. How could you? You know absolutely nothing about me, nothing about my past.

So why did he make her think of it? Remember things she'd rather let cobwebs grow over? No boyfriends because her one experience of the opposite sex had left her jaundiced enough never to test the water again.

Eric Dean, who had lied about his age, lied about his marital status, lied about his job, lied about everything it was possible to lie about. And she hadn't seen behind the lies until it had been too late and she'd been foolishly pregnant.

'I find that rather sad,' he commented.

'My house is just at the end of this road. On the right, just beyond the letter box.' She absolutely refused to have him fish information out of her as a way of passing the time and making small talk. She had always been deeply guarded of her private life, and she wasn't about to let that guard drop now, even though for a second there she had felt a strange pull to confide. Peculiar. But then they said that it was often easier to confide in complete strangers than in the people who knew you intimately.

'Well,' she said, when they had pulled up outside the house, 'thank you for putting yourself out and arranging this dinner.' Should she shake his hand, or was that a bit too businesslike? Since she didn't want to feel the coolness of his skin against hers anyway, she kept her hands firmly clasped together on her lap. 'You had no need to, and I appreciate that.'

'What about a nightcap?'

'A what…?'

He didn't answer. Instead, he opened his door, swung his long body out, and Jessica very hurriedly followed suit.

'I'm afraid I don't keep a great deal of alcohol in the house,' she stammered, thinking that his overall impression of her, based on one night in the company of two teenagers, was probably of a dull 'stay at home' woman with nothing else to fill her life apart from her daughter. Then she immediately decided that she didn't care what he thought anyway, which made her feel much better.

'A cup of coffee would be fine.'

'A cup of coffee.' Jessica fumbled with the door key then finally got the damned thing to work. 'Sure,' she said, pushing the door open and switching on the hall lights.

She walked through to the sitting room, assuming that he was following her, but when she did finally look at him, he was gazing around him with appreciation.

'Charming,' he said eventually, his eyes meeting hers.

'That's the sort of word that estate agents use when they want to describe somewhere incredibly small which has been brightened up by a spot of floral wallpaper.'

'Do you *ever* accept a compliment at face value? Or do you argue about *everything*?' He shoved his hands in his pockets and stood there, inspecting her thoroughly.

Jessica didn't know what to say. He had tried to be pleasant and polite, and had been met with a cold rebuff. Though not deliberately. I'm not used to this, she thought with surprise. I'm not used to a man being inside this house, I'm not used to being complimented, I'm not used to feeling awkward and defensive in front of someone else.

'I'm sorry I snapped. I must be a little tired.' She could tell that he didn't believe her because he raised his eyebrows and continued to stare at her in silence. Okay, she thought irritably, so I overreacted. So sue me!

'How do you take your coffee?'

'Black, two sugars.'

To her consternation, he followed her into the kitchen and promptly sat down at the table, watching as she made them both a mug of coffee.

'Feel free to describe my kitchen as charming,' she said, trying to make up for her response to his compliment earlier on. 'I promise I won't bite your head off.' She handed him the mug and primly sat opposite him.

It felt odd, this. Sitting here at this hour of the night, at the kitchen table, talking to this man. Every so often, she had friends from work over. It was always very casual—pasta at the kitchen table, a bottle or two of wine, some music. It never felt like this.

'How long have you lived here?'

'Years. I like it. It's convenient for where I work, and I've spent time on it.' That was almost approaching a confidence, and out of habit she pulled back and took a sip of coffee. 'You mentioned that you wanted to chat about this evening.'

'Was it what you had hoped for?' He looked at her carefully over the rim of his cup.

Jessica gave that some thought, and then said, with a shrug, 'I'm not sure what I'd hoped for. I guess that my mind's been set at rest insofar as Mark seems a pleasant enough boy…'

'You'd expected long hair? An earring? A cigarette permanently glued to his lower lip?'

'I couldn't imagine what he'd be like,' Jessica said warily. She fidgeted in the chair and concentrated on the mug of coffee. Over the sound of the ticking of the wall clock she could hear the fast, furious beating of her heart. Whatever lectures she gave herself, something inside her responded to this man and it was sufficient to send her into a state of panic.

'Still think that it might be a good idea for me to warn him away from your daughter?'

'I suppose not.' If anything, Mark had seemed a stabilising influence, and it disturbed her to realise that she had misread a situation so comprehensively.

'You'll probably jump onto the defensive if I tell you this, but if you're looking for answers to Lucy's behaviour then I suggest you get them from her. She's responsible for her own actions, for her own behaviour.'

'She's only a child! How can you say that?' Her cheeks felt inflamed with colour.

'She's no longer quite the child she once was, I imagine. She's growing up. It was bound to happen, you know.'

'Are you giving me a lecture on my own daughter?' Jessica stared at the loathsome man, aghast.

'I'm telling you what I think, from a completely detached point of view.'

'Good of you!' she retorted sarcastically. 'Any more sweeping generalisations, while you're about it?'

His lips tightened and he drained the remainder of his coffee in one gulp.

'You're not going to let anyone give you advice, are you?' he asked coolly. 'You can be on the verge of stepping over the edge, but, if someone points that out, you'll go right ahead and do it anyway, because you don't need help or suggestions from anyone.'

'That's not true! How dare you come here and then...' She had to take a deep breath because she could feel herself losing control of her voice. 'And then proceed to psychoanalyse me?'

'I'm doing no such thing, although, admittedly, you'd make a great case study.'

'And what exactly is *that* supposed to mean?' She stared defiantly at him. Her hands were shaking, her voice was shaking, her face was red. Where had all her self-control gone? She had a child of sixteen! She should be able to act in a more reasoned and mature manner than this.

'What happened to Lucy's father?'

The directness of the question caught her unawares, and she looked at him as though he had dared to ask her the most personal and insulting of questions, such as the colour of her underwear or what size bra she wore.

'At a guess,' he continued, in the face of her silence, 'I'd say that for whatever reason he flew the coop probably before Lucy was even born. At a guess, I'd say that you've spent the past sixteen years making sure that no one breaks through that veneer of yours.'

'Oh, is that a fact?' She frankly couldn't think of anything else to say. Words, arguments, any kind of coherent vocabulary, had deserted her in the face of such an overwhelming intrusion of her privacy. Overwhelming and uninvited.

'Are you going to deny it?'

'I don't have to deny anything! And while we're on the subject of perfect parenting...'' Sheer, hysterical emotion was about to take over. Jessica could feel it in every pore of her body, but she was powerless to resist the urge to fly off the handle. 'It doesn't seem to me that you're exactly the ideal father figure yourself! It's fine for you to waltz in here and then proceed to tell me what I'm doing wrong...' Just the thought of it was enough to make her face burn. She didn't care whether he had a point or not. She quite simply felt as though her lifetime's work had been derided in the space of five minutes. 'But you and Mark aren't exactly a shining example of the great bond between father and son!'

'No. We aren't.'

His admission was enough to take the wind out of her sails. She had overreacted. So he had made his hurtful observations, but there had been nothing malicious behind them. She had responded with a cheap desire to retaliate, whatever the cost.

'I think it's probably best for me to leave now.' He stood up, a huge, commanding figure, dwarfing the little kitchen, and Jessica sprang to her feet almost simultaneously.

'There's no need... I'm awfully sorry...'

'Whatever for?' There was no warmth in his voice, and he began heading out of the kitchen.

It occurred to her that this would probably be the last time that she would ever lay eyes on him, and, infuriating though he had proved, the prospect of that was like being punched in the stomach.

Of course, it was because he would walk away with completely the wrong impression of her. He would leave thinking that she was a wilful, stubborn, unpleasant, pigheaded fool.

'I'm sorry about mentioning your relationship with your son.' She reached out and touched his arm very gently, and he stopped. Immediately Jessica let her hand drop to her side. She could feel her fingers tingling where they had come into contact with his jacket. 'It was rude and uncalled for,' she said bravely.

He smiled slowly. 'In that case, I won't give you detention,' he said in his low, deep, utterly mesmerising voice. 'But I really still have to get home. For a start I don't think that Mark took a key with him. Someone might hear him yelling at a locked front door and call the police.'

He headed towards the door and Jessica followed in his wake. So, will I be seeing you again? she stupidly wanted to ask.

'Well,' she said instead, opening the front door and

standing back, 'I hope Mark does well in his exams and gets into university.'

'I'll tell him you said that.'

'Oh, no, then he might think that we carried on chatting after they left!'

'True! What a horrifying thought!' Then another glimpse of one of those rare, amused, captivating smiles, and he was gone.

The space he left seemed disproportionately large. Jessica busied herself in the kitchen, tidying away the mugs, surprised when Lucy returned home in high spirits and well before the witching hour.

So. He'd been right about that, at any rate. Letting her go to the wretched nightclub had circumvented at least an hour's worth of bickering and had done wonders for her daughter's spirits.

What else had he been right about?

CHAPTER FOUR

'MARK seems a very nice boy.'

Jessica knew that any such observation had to be made with precision timing. Too soon after the prearranged dinner would have been instantly put down to maternal nosiness, too long after and, knowing Lucy, she would have completely forgotten the episode.

Jessica gave it a couple of days, and, when nothing was forthcoming, she decided to mention the dinner, but casually, at the weekend, sitting in front of the television while Lucy sat next to her on the sofa and divided her time between scathing comments on the documentary they were watching, glancing at a school test, and yawning dramatically.

'I hate that description "nice",' Lucy said absent-mindedly. 'It's the sort of word people use to describe cream cakes.'

'Interesting, then.'

'More interesting than those childish idiots in my class at school, at any rate.'

'Where did you meet him? You never said.'

'Tennis match.'

'Tennis match?' Jessica had never heard mention of any tennis match. As far as she was aware Lucy dabbled occasionally with a tennis racquet, but there was no way that she was up to competitive tennis. Not unless she had secretly been taking lessons, which was unlikely since most forms of sport tended to provoke scathing criticism.

'School arranged it.' She yawned widely, looked at her mother and grinned. 'Pretty funny, too. All the people from Mark's school turned up wearing the regulation starched white outfits. All of us turned up in whatever we could manage to grab from the wardrobe before we left home. Mrs Talbot was furious!' Lucy beamed a little wider at the memory of that. 'She said that we were an insult to the school.'

'Oh, Lucy!' Jessica sighed, and decided that she really should say something at this point. 'You should have told me. We could have gone out and bought you a little white skirt.'

'No way! I would have stuck out like a sore thumb.'

'Yes, but…'

'Anyway, splashing out on a little white tennis outfit that I'd have worn once would have been a waste of money, and you keep saying that we're poor.'

'I do *not* keep saying that, Luce, and we don't have to count pennies quite so vigorously.' But she could see Lucy's point. She had made a habit of being careful. There had been no choice. No spending sprees, a cheap and cheerful fortnight's holiday once a year—usually to Cornwall—clothes that were utilitarian for herself rather than decorative.

'You know what I mean.'

Since this seemed to be straying from the topic, Jessica said, on a placatory note, 'So, who won the tennis match?'

'They did! Most of us could hardly play, though we put up a good fight.'

'And you played against Mark?'

'Why so interested?'

'It's just…' she refrained from using the word 'nice' '..helpful for me to know who your friends are.' She paused. 'Anyway, I'm glad I met him. As I said, he seems a very down to earth kind of boy.'

'I've told you, Mum—he's not a *boy*. He's seventeen!'

'Sorry—young man. The sort of boy that any girl would be proud to bring home to show her mother.' Jessica didn't think that she had heard herself make such an infuriatingly fuddy-duddy remark in her life before. She very nearly groaned out loud. This was what it did to you, she thought—having a child at the age of seventeen, with no support systems to fall back on, catapulted you straight out of childhood into adulthood without the benefit of any build up in between.

And, in a way, it had been worse for her because she had spent the past sixteen-odd years locked in her self-imposed ivory tower. Oh, she had her friends, and they were great fun, but the companionship of a man, the warmth of someone else's laughter in bed at night, had been missing from her life. She had voluntarily given it all up because she had been afraid of being hurt again, afraid of trusting, once she had discovered that trust could be broken, and in the most cavalier of ways.

Eric Dean had done that to her; that had been his final parting gift.

She felt a sudden, shocking flare of bitterness and resentment.

How could he have betrayed her trust so completely? He had created a plausible persona for himself, and it had all been a charade to get her into bed. As it had turned out, it had been a matter of force on his part and fear on hers. Even thinking about it now made her feel sick.

But still—until now—she had happily justified her seclusion, happily viewed other people's complex love lives with a certain amount of relief—relief that she was not part of any of it. Recently, though... Well, had she been wrong?

Lucy was talking, telling her that she was becoming a one-woman dictatorship. 'Anyway,' she said without guile, 'Mark and I aren't *going out*. We see one another, sure, but we're not involved in *that* way.'

'You're not?' Jessica forgot her brief surge of introspection. This was the first time that Lucy had mentioned anything to do with her love life, or absence of one. 'Not, of course, that I don't expect you to have a love life...a boyfriend...whatever...' Who am I kidding? she thought. Deep down, I don't expect her to have any love life, least of all a sex life, until she's well into her twenties and knows what she's going to do with the rest of her life.

Lucy didn't reply, but she was staring hard at the television screen, eyes averted, cheeks pink.

'Just as long as you take the necessary precautions...' How was it that this subject had never been broached before? A couple of years ago, she had explained about the birds and the bees and that had been easy. A technical chat about babies and where they came from, all fairly pointless, as it turned out, since Lucy knew more on the subject from a purely biological point of view than Jessica did.

But this—mentioning contraception, discussing sex and the possibility of it—it made her feel helpless and lost.

'Oh, Mum, p...l...ease...'

'Well, darling...'

'Don't worry! I'm not about to hop into bed with Mark Newman! If anything, you should be grateful that I know him at all—he's the only one who's trying to persuade me to go on to sixth form. Apart from you, that is, and those dreary teachers at school. If they're any kind of example of what'll become of me if I stay on at school, then I'd rather look for work at a supermarket.'

'You don't mean that, Lucy.' And she didn't. It was all a show of bravado. At the last parents' evening, she had got glowing reports from all her teachers who had been full of praise.

Still, it was disturbing, this recurring theme of Lucy's—the threat that she would leave school and do some kind of course. There was, after all, no smoke without a fire.

'Why not? You did, and I know you complain that you could have done more, but you have a pretty good job. There are graduates all over the country who are out of work, who'd kill to do what you're doing.'

'And there are graduates all over the country who are climbing steadily upwards,' Jessica said quickly, but any signs of interest in the conversation from Lucy were fast vanishing. The documentary had finished. A hospital drama had started—much more gripping to judge from the expression on her daughter's face. She had always been fascinated with blood, operations and the mystique of medicine.

'Shh, Mum…I want to watch this…'

'Have you finished your homework?'

'In a minute.'

'Lucy…!'

'It's only maths—I can do it with my eyes closed.'

Which was true enough. As far as maths and sciences went, she absorbed knowledge like a sponge, and could store an amazing array of technical information.

Jessica sighed and stared vacantly at the television screen, but her thoughts were a thousand miles away.

Kath would not be going on to do her A levels. Nor would Robin. Their parents had not expected them to, and weren't in the least disappointed. These girls were Lucy's closest friends, and peer pressure was a powerful thing.

Mark Newman and his tenuous encouragement of Lucy's education now seemed positively advantageous. She wished that she had been thinking on her feet at the time, had perhaps suggested that he pop over for dinner, made a definite date, even though it was doubtful that Lucy would have appreciated the gesture.

If only his father had been a little warmer, a little more *human-like* and a little less downright forbidding, she might have been tempted to give him a call, but she dismissed the thought even before it had begun to take root.

His impact on her had not diminished since she had last seen him on Thursday. If anything, it had become stronger. She could hardly venture into her own kitchen now without remembering how he'd dwarfed it with his lean, towering body. She could remember his overpowering presence as vividly as she could recall the colour of his hair and the shade of his eyes.

To say the least, it was irritating.

It also seemed to dominate her life more than was appropriate. A brief interlude with a man who had been cornered into helping her had no right to become anything more than a passing memory with time.

It hardly helped matters either that, having met Mark Newman and ascertained that he was just the sort of influence that Lucy needed, his name seemed to have been abruptly dropped from Lucy's conversation.

That, she supposed, had always been the danger. Had legitimising him somehow removed the glamour for Lucy? Turned him into someone boring who wore jackets occasionally and could converse in adult company? With her *mother*, of all people?

It was a pleasant relief when, three weeks later, Adam Chauncy, her boss, asked her out to lunch. It was during Secretary Week. This was one of those inventions masterminded years back to maintain a happy working environment. For one week during the year, the secretaries were all taken out by their bosses for lunch to a restaurant of their choosing, as a gesture of thanks for hard work.

It had begun when the firm had been younger and smaller. They had gone out as a group then, but now, with several expansions under its belt, the group idea was no longer feasible and the week had somehow grown into a fortnight, so that the bosses could make time to take the senior secretaries out on a one-to-one basis.

'Where would you like to go?' Adam asked her, on the Monday.

'Money no object?' Jessica teased. Adam was fifty-two years old and a dear.

'I absolutely put my foot down at a plane trip to Paris for the day.'

'Well, that limits my options, in that case.' Jessica laughed and then said suddenly, 'I know a nice spot, though. Not in the West End. A little French restaurant—super atmosphere.' She had been impressed with the food, with the service, with the decor, and when else would she get the chance to pay a second visit? No point telling herself that she would splash out and treat herself and Lucy to another meal there. She knew that when the time came she would chicken out at the thought of the whopping bill at the end of it.

So later in the week she found herself again dressing for Chez Jacques, albeit with no nervous fluttering in the pit of her stomach this time.

The weather had become hotter over the past few weeks. Very soon the authorities would announce a hose-pipe ban, something that Jessica found amusing whenever she glanced into her back garden. It was so compact that a hose would probably convert it into a swimming pool.

It was warm enough, though, for her to wear her pale green sleeveless shift, without the regulatory jacket which seemed to be part of her working wardrobe, whatever the weather. Sitting out in the garden at the weekends had put a tawny glow on her cheeks, and her blonde hair was streaked into natural highlights. She didn't *look* mumsy, she decided, staring at her reflection in the mirror and daring it to challenge the observation. She might *feel* it most of the time, but right now she felt young and attractive.

She perversely thought of Anthony Newman and wished that he could see her now. Glowing from the sun rather than hassled with worries about Lucy.

So it was with shock, halfway through the meal, as she was listening to Adam hold forth on two of his cases which were proving more laborious than he had initially anticipated, that she glanced up and saw none other than Anthony Newman being shown to a table.

He was not dressed for work. His clothes were casual, well tailored and clearly expensive. His moss-green polo shirt bore an emblem on one side, and she would bet a year's salary that it wasn't a department store logo.

Adam's conversation suddenly lost all interest value. She continued to nod, murmur and shake her head in the right places, but she knew that she had slunk down a little lower in her chair, and was eagerly and compulsively absorbing the sight of Anthony Newman at the table. He was obviously waiting for someone.

Natural curiosity, she told herself. Human nature at work.

Having idly reflected earlier that morning that she wouldn't have minded him seeing her relaxed, tanned and without a teenager in tow, she now realised that the last person she wanted to lay eyes on was him.

Fortunately, with a little repositioning of herself, Adam successfully blocked most of her from view.

It helped as well that the restaurant was full—not that he was paying the slightest bit of notice to anything around him. He had brought a document folder with him, and had proceeded to extract a slim wad of papers which he was now perusing, frowning and making notes. Ever at work, she thought.

She dragged her attention away from him long enough to make a few intelligent responses to what Adam was saying, and then found her eyes drifting back towards the casually impressive figure at the table. Of course, she should really make her presence known. Politeness dictated it, if nothing else, but she knew that she had no intention of doing any such thing.

Firstly because the thought of his eyes on her, assessing, made her squirm with discomfort. And, secondly, because she instinctively reacted against giving the wrong impression—what if he thought that she was being pushy? She realised with a little dismay that she had lost the art of relating to men. She was fine in a work environment, or in a group, but on a one-to-one basis she had grown rusty over time.

For experience, she could only substitute her imagination, and her imagination told her that a man like Anthony Newman would probably be a little aghast at being approached by a woman whose presence had originally been forced onto him, and whom he had probably quite forgotten. It would be mortifying.

She reverted her attention to Adam, making sure that she smiled a lot, responded a lot, and acted in a normal manner. But, even with eyes heavily averted, she still managed to see the woman who was eventually shown to Anthony's table.

How could she fail to notice her? Nearly everyone else in the restaurant did. There was the discreet turning of heads as they watched the easy, confident stride of the six-foot blonde. Short hair, short skirt, long, long legs. A figure built for a catwalk.

She had wondered what sort of women Anthony Newman was attracted to. Now she knew. Elegant, refined, beautiful and young. This particular model couldn't have been older than her early twenties.

'You're much better looking, my dear,' Adam said, patting her hand, and Jessica blushed madly.

'Adam Chauncy, I was *not*...'

'Course you were! My wife does it all the time. She says that it's a healthy female reaction to check the competition.'

Jessica laughed. 'Your wife hasn't *got* any competition.'

'I know,' Adam said comfortably, 'and I wouldn't be too surprised if she knew it as well. And, my dear—' he leant forward and whispered confidentially '—you should be quite confident that that child isn't a patch on you. You have a far more interesting face.'

'*Interesting?* I'm not entirely sure that "interesting" is the sort of look that most women would kill for...' But she laughed anyway, and threw him an affectionate look.

At least, she decided, he hadn't told her that she had a lived-in look. One of her friends had told her that her husband had made the mistake of paying her that particular compliment and she had instantly tipped a plate of salad on his lap, complete with dressing.

Adam was settling the bill, and the waiter returned with his credit card and a note. A note for her. Of course, she knew what it was the instant she took it from the tray. Who else would be sending her a note in a restaurant? Who else in the restaurant *knew* her?

She read it, smiled frozenly as her mind blanked out for a couple of seconds, and then explained that someone across the room had recognised her.

'Who?'

'The man who just happens to be sitting with the eye-catching blonde whose looks aren't a patch on mine.'

'Really?'

'He's asked me to join them for a cup of coffee. Adam, if you don't mind waiting for a few minutes while I say hello, I'll just inform him that I can't possibly as I've got to return to work.'

'Nonsense!' He smiled at her. 'Today's special. You're a damn fine worker, Jessie, and no lunch can repay you enough for the years of dedication you've put into the company. You just go along for that cup of coffee and take your time. Half the afternoon's gone already, anyway!'

'No, really, Adam, there are a few things...'

'Have a break, my dear!'

Maybe another day, she wanted to tell him. Any other day.

'But...'

'No buts! You can pop in to work if you like a bit later, but personally I don't think there's much point. You live just around here, Jessie. Take the afternoon off!' He stood up and said briskly, 'Now, off you go!'

Jessie looked at him with alarm. She didn't *want* to go anywhere! Apart from in the direction of the office.

She plastered a smile on her face and walked briskly across to where Anthony and his girlfriend were sitting. It was every bit as nerve-racking as she had anticipated. He looked at her as she approached with an assessing directness that very nearly bordered on insolence but somehow managed to stop just short. And the blonde, who close up looked even younger, followed the direction of his gaze, but suspiciously.

'Jessica!' He stood up as she sat down on the chair which a waiter had obligingly pulled out for her. 'I wondered whether you'd spotted us over here.'

'No! I was...too busy listening to my lunch companion...!'

'This is Fiona Charleton.' His voice was thick with charm, and Jessica had a sneaking feeling that she was missing something. 'An old friend of the family.'

Twenty-two, Jessica thought, if not younger. What on earth was Anthony Newman doing with a child who was almost young enough to be his daughter? Who was, in fact, probably only a handful of years older than *her own* daughter?

She smiled stiffly, shook the thin, cool hand, and hoped that neither of them would see the disapproval in her eyes.

Perhaps this thing went on all the time in rich, fast circles. Who knew? Perhaps Anthony Newman liked the uncomplicated subservience of youth—the blank sheet of paper waiting to be written on.

'And how long have you known Anthony?' Jessica asked politely, making sure that she didn't look at him, although she could feel his eyes on her.

'Years…' Large, limpid blue eyes drifted adoringly in the direction of Anthony.

'Like I said,' he said hastily, 'Fiona's a family friend. A neighbour, as a matter of fact.'

'In London?'

'Warwickshire. Her family had a house next to ours. Coffee?'

'Really, I can't stay.' She forced herself to face him, and felt the full impact of his overpowering, masculine charm. Whatever he was radiating, it was lethal, particularly as she had no inkling as to the reason for its abundance. 'I have to get back to work.' She looked significantly at her watch and wondered whether it would be ridiculous to exclaim something along the lines of Oh, is that the time?

'I'm sure your boss could spare you for a few minutes.' He didn't give her time to debate the point. He signalled a waiter over and a cup of black coffee was in front of her virtually before she could protest.

'And how's Lucy?' Quick glance in the direction of Fiona. 'Lucy is a good friend of Mark.'

Fiona seemed to be working this one out. It has to be said, Jessica thought, that, beautiful though the package might be, not much seems to be happening in the head. He clearly liked his women fairly vacant and undemanding.

'Fine.' She looked him over coldly. 'And Mark?'

'Fine.' He paused. 'Glad I bumped into you, as a matter of fact,' he said, sipping his coffee, his body slightly inclined away from the table.

'You are?'

'Absolutely.' He smiled a devastating smile that had Jessica diving into her cup of coffee for refuge.

Whatever was going on with her body? Her heart felt as though it was about to burst, and her skin was hot and uncomfortable. She smiled at Fiona, reminding herself that this was the sort of beauty that attracted a man like Anthony Newman. Glamorous as opposed to interesting. 'And do you work, Fiona?' she asked. Any vacuous question to take her mind off this alarming effect he was having on her.

Fiona frowned, as if trying to puzzle this one out. Work? her face seemed to be saying. What on earth is that?

'Do you have a job?' Jessica asked helpfully.

'Oh, yes.' The smooth, alabaster-white face cleared into a dazzling smile. Really, Jessica thought, she should be a model.

'I do. I work at my godfather's gallery twice a week. It's super, really, because he gives me as much time off as I want for holidays!'

'You go on holiday a lot?' The conversation seemed to be getting surreal. She wished that Anthony would join in and rescue her—after all, the woman was *his* lunch companion—but he seemed quite happy to remain silent. She glanced in his direction and saw that he was, if anything, vaguely amused, which made her want to click her tongue in annoyance.

'Oh, yes!' Fiona's face lit up with another radiant smile. 'Skiing every winter, then there's tennis, and

Henley. And Mustique for summer. Mummy and Daddy own a house there. It's super!'

Jessica felt a little faint at this glib description of a life that was so far removed from her own. Or anyone else's that she knew, for that matter.

'Fiona doesn't consider work an essential part of life,' Anthony drawled, though not unkindly. 'Do you, Fi?'

'Well, I quite like the gallery…' She pouted, which reminded Jessica of Lucy, except that Lucy's pouts tended to look rather more sullen. 'But I don't suppose I shall ever have a *real* job.'

'What do you mean by a 'real' job?' Jessica asked, lost.

'Oh…' Perfectly shaped brows met in a fleeting frown. 'I mean something where I would have to get up before nine and stay until after three.'

'Oh, one of those!' Jessica was about to make a sarcastic rejoinder to that little observation, but the simple innocence on Fiona's face made any such temptation almost seem criminal. Thank God Lucy wasn't around, Jessica thought; she would have eaten this poor girl for breakfast in under thirty seconds. She felt a warm flow of deep love for her daughter.

'Anyway,' Anthony's deep voice said from alongside her, 'you still haven't asked me why I'm so pleased to have bumped into you.'

There was no choice. Jessica turned slightly and looked at him, and immediately felt another one of those little electric frissons of awareness shoot up her spine.

The sun over the past few weeks had worked wonders on him as well. His skin was bronzed. He didn't look like someone who worked in an office. He looked like someone who worked on a yacht—out in the open somewhere, doing something vigorous that built up muscle and body tone. Any wonder Fiona seemed to be hanging onto his every gesture? He probably ran circles round all the young, beautiful things in his social set, not to mention the older, less beautiful ones.

It was just as well that she was inured to that kind of obvious charm and good looks. Eric had been good-looking too. A good-looking bounder, as he would have been known decades ago, with an edge of real cruelty that he had cleverly kept hidden at the start.

She shook her head to clear it of unwelcome thoughts. What on earth was wrong with her? She hadn't given that no-good cad this much attention in years!

'I'm sorry, I hadn't realised that it was a question waiting for an answer.' Her voice sounded normal, polite. Thank heavens.

'I would have called you, actually...'

'Would you?' Jessica frowned suspiciously at him. She almost wished that he was as cold and distant as he had been the first time she had met him. Cold and distant she could deal with.

'Mark and I are going to Elmsden on the weekend. How would you and Lucy like to come along?'

'Elmsden?' She gaped at him in utter confusion.

'Anthony...! You *promised* that you would take me up with you the next time you went! You know how much I adore it there...!'

'It's purely a utilitarian visit, Fi,' he said kindly to the distraught girl whose eyes were glazing over with tears. She blinked rapidly and gazed miserably down into her coffee.

Jessica, for reasons unknown, felt like an ogre, even though she had done nothing to provoke this obvious show of disappointment.

'I really don't think...'

'Elmsden's my parents' country house. They no longer live there. They retired to sunny isles about four years ago, but it's fallen to me to make sure that it keeps ticking over, so I do my duty once every six weeks or so…' He smiled at her, and she had a passing sensation of dizziness. 'I thought that you and Lucy might enjoy the break.'

'Because we're forced by circumstances to remain cooped up in London?' Jessica said stiffly, and the smile was replaced by a quick frown.

'Actually, that wasn't the reason.'

'No?' It was almost a relief to be having an argument, though she couldn't understand why.

'Oh, Ants, if Francesca doesn't want to go…'

'Jessica,' said Jessica.

'Then let's you and I go together. We'll have a wonderful time! It's so hot and stuffy here in London at the moment, and you know how divine it is there. We could laze around the pool, doing nothing…' She gazed at him pleadingly, and Jessica smiled in turn, encouraging him to accept the simple request.

It was as if Fiona hadn't spoken. His attention was focused solely on Jessica. She could feel the intensity of it draining her.

'To be honest,' he said lazily, 'I thought that Mark and Lucy might benefit from it.' He shrugged lightly. 'Of course, if you don't agree…'

Jessica thought rapidly. Hadn't she spent the past few weeks bemoaning the fact that she hadn't actively encouraged Mark? Hadn't she been pleasantly surprised at how stable, well adjusted and normal he was? And this coming weekend couldn't have been a better one. Lucy had been making noises about vanishing on the Saturday for a party—an all-night party—which had sent shivers down Jessica's spine.

A weekend in the country, she thought, where Lucy would be out of harm's way, and where Mark would have some undiluted time to preach his gospel on the wisdom of continuing her education. True, there was the drawback of having Anthony around, but there was nothing to fear from that quarter. He had a girlfriend and, even if he hadn't, he was as uninterested in her as a fish was uninterested in discovering what lay outside the pond.

And from her point of view he was no threat. Her pulses might speed up whenever her eyes happened to tangle with his, but she could handle it. She had spent years mastering the art of handling men.

And, besides, Mark and Lucy would be around, and knowing her daughter there wouldn't be a moment's peace. For all her pretence at maturity, Lucy still had the clinginess of a child.

'Yes, it might be a very nice idea...' she said slowly, and she glanced apologetically and reassuringly at Fiona. 'If I could explain. Lucy, my daughter...'

'Oh, Fiona would be bored rigid by explanations,' he said, waving his hand in a dismissive manner. He summoned the waiter for the bill, and while they were waiting offered, in a placatory way, to spend the rest of the afternoon dragging himself around Harrods, if that was how Fiona wanted to occupy herself.

'Not,' he added, 'that your parents will love that idea, when the bills come back to them.'

But it worked. Fiona looked cheered at this, and, with some chagrin, Jessica realised that the child obviously had no jealousy of her whatsoever.

Still, it was too late to back down now, and at the end of the day it was a good idea. Wasn't it?

He turned to her as they stood outside the restaurant, getting their bearings, and said in a low, amused voice, 'Now, don't forget—I shall pick you both up on Saturday morning at nine-thirty. That way we can have as much of the weekend as possible.'

Jessica felt a few doubts settle in, but she politely smiled them away.

Nine-thirty. Saturday morning. Yes, it might well do that stubborn daughter of hers a world of good.

CHAPTER FIVE

JESSICA waited until Friday evening before she broke the news about Anthony's invitation.

She gallantly told herself that this had nothing to do with cowardice. She was merely giving herself time to work out whether she really wanted to go at all. What had seemed a good enough idea at the time had gradually become less and less inviting.

Theoretically, yes, it made sense—throw Mark and Lucy together, and his stabilising influence *must* wear off on her after a while. A process of osmosis.

On the other hand, might not the whole idea work against her? Mark as the creative rebel, pursuing a career against his father's wishes, might appeal. Mark, however, as champion of her mother's causes might hold considerably less appeal.

The more Jessica worried at the question, the more uncertain she felt about the whole thing.

But then, a change of mind would involve the fuss of having to get in touch with Anthony Newman and make her apologies, and that held even less appeal.

So a vacillating frame of mind took her to the end of the week until cancelling was out of the question without appearing out-and-out rude.

She waited until Lucy was beginning to nod off in front of the television before she made her announcement. It was still only nine-thirty—surprisingly early— but she had discovered that Lucy, while capable of partying until the wee hours of the morning, seemed to

81

spend most of her time in a state of perpetual drowsiness.

'Oh, Luce!' she said, looking up from the newspaper and rousing her daughter from near slumber. 'I forgot to tell you, but guess who I bumped into at that little French restaurant I went to with Adam?'

'Miss Evans, roaringly drunk and doing a striptease on a table?'

Miss Evans was the school principal, a spinster in her fifties who ruled the school with a rod of iron. Personally, Jessica felt that she was single-handedly responsible for the high calibre of the teachers and the academic success of the school. Lucy, on the other hand, frequently complained that she had missed a promising career as a prison warden.

'Anthony Newman,' she said, ignoring Lucy's remark.

'Who's Anthony Newman?'

Jessica sighed and looked at her daughter with fond exasperation. There were times when she wondered whether Lucy was connected to planet earth at all.

'Mark Newman's father. Remember him? We met them at that very same restaurant a few weeks ago.'

'Oh, yes.' She tucked her legs under her and appeared to lose interest in the conversation.

'Anyway,' Jessica persevered patiently, 'we had a little chat, and…'

'I think it's very odd that you ran into that man. Are you following him?' Lucy gave a little snort of amusement at this.

'It's not really that odd,' Jessica replied sharply. 'It's obviously a favourite haunt of his.'

'Some haunt. Most people's favourite haunts are their local pubs. Well, Mark did say that he's one of a kind.'

She managed to make this sound as though 'one of a kind' implied an undesirable alien of sorts.

'He's invited us to go and spend a weekend with them at their country house. He's coming to collect us to-morrow morning.'

At this Lucy sat up as though she had been struck by a bolt of lightning. The drowsy, semi-bored expression had given way to a ferocious scowl.

'No way! You can go if you like, but I can't go. There's a party tomorrow night, and Robin—'

'You're not going to any party,' Jessica said quietly. 'I accepted his invitation on behalf of both of us, and you're coming along if I have to drag you there kicking and screaming.'

'But, Mum! I *have* to go to that party! It's one in a lifetime! It's an open-air rock concert, and it's only go-ing to be on for that one night!'

Open-air rock concert? Jessica had an image of un-savoury, long-haired men, and girls dressed in next to nothing, steadily consuming alcohol and Lord only knew what else. You go to that sort of thing over my dead body, she was tempted to say. Instead, she smiled and moderated her voice.

'Well, you'll just have to give it a miss, Luce.'

'I can't!'

'It's not the end of the world. There'll be another open-air concert some time…'

'The same could be said for a weekend in the country. I can't imagine how he's managed to drag Mark along to that…'

'Lucy. No arguments. I want you to go upstairs and pack a bag. There's a pool, apparently, so you can take your swimsuit with you…'

'But, *Mum*…!'

'I'm not about to give in, Luce. It'll do us both good to get out of London for a couple of days. It's so hot here, and—'

'I *hate* the countryside! It's boring. What are we going to do for a whole *weekend* there? Take long, bracing walks, I suppose? Have chummy singsongs around the grand piano in the evening?'

The thought of Anthony Newman indulging in singsongs around a grand piano was so comical that Jessica looked down to hide the laughter she felt rising up inside.

'It'll be fun,' she said, plastering a serious expression on her face. 'And won't it be nice to be surrounded by fields and countryside? Wouldn't it make a change from dirty streets and traffic and buildings?'

She assumed that Elmsden wasn't located in the middle of a housing estate.

Lucy was staring at her as though she had taken leave of her senses. 'Are you sure that this wondrous invitation wasn't for *your* benefit?' she asked suspiciously. Her thoughts had swerved off on a tangent and she was scrutinising her mother now. 'I mean, you're not *that* old, and, really, you're not bad-looking for someone of your age…'

'Thanks, Luce,' Jessica said dryly. 'Any more compliments up your sleeve?'

'W…e…ll, you know what I mean…' She had forgotten about the all-night party, or rock concert, or whatever. She was now on the scent of something else, and Jessica didn't know whether to be relieved or alarmed by this change of direction.

'Anyway, darling…' she said briskly, rattling her newspaper to indicate the end of the conversation.

'I mean, he's not bad-looking either, for someone of his age...'

'*Lucy!*'

'Mark said that his dad always has a string of glamour girls around him, so he must have *something*...'

'Don't be ridiculous!' Jessica wasn't accustomed to being questioned on her love life, even if Lucy's questions *were* way off line. She had never *had* a love life. She realised that she found her daughter's inquisition a bit embarrassing.

'Why is it ridiculous?' Lucy insisted, with the tenacity of a bloodhound on the trail of something tasty. 'You've never had a boyfriend, Mum. And don't tell me that there haven't been opportunities. You remember that oddball a year and a half ago? Gerry something or other? With the goofy smile? Used to phone you up all the time?'

Jessica could feel her face getting red. 'He was a very nice man, Luce...'

'Then how come you gave him the brush-off?'

At the time Jessica had never imagined that Lucy had been paying the slightest interest in that particular little occurrence. She had met Gerry through a friend of a friend, at a Christmas party, and for a while he had pursued her avidly. But she hadn't been interested. Not at all. He was likeable enough, and politeness had obliged her to accept one dinner invitation with him, but then she had had to firmly inform him that she had no interest in taking their acquaintanceship further. Now it amazed her that Lucy had stored up the episode, when at the time she had seemed not in the least interested.

'He just wasn't my...my type, I suppose you could say,' Jessica mumbled vaguely.

'So who *is* your type?'

'Lucy!'

'Well, you're always asking me about *my* social life.'

'That's different! You're my daughter!'

'And you're my mother!'

'You would make a very successful barrister, Luce, do you know that? Anyway, just throw a few things in your bag—a few sensible things that no one can find over-offensive.'

Lucy seemed to find this idea amusing, because she grinned. 'Okay.'

'Okay?' There was an element of surprise in Jessica's voice. Whatever had happened to the argument about the party? She was immensely relieved that it had been dropped, but she was stunned by the speed of her daughter's change of mind. But then, wasn't that typical Luce? She was as changeable as the weather on a spring day.

Of course, she was back to complaining in undertones the following morning as they polished off a light breakfast and waited for Anthony to arrive.

Jessica, rather than lose her temper, took refuge in house cleaning, while Lucy followed in her wake, mumbling about what she would be missing, darkly implying that her entire life would be scarred by missing this one rock concert.

Jessica ignored the moaning, but she was frankly relieved when she heard the doorbell ring.

'Now,' she said sternly, 'I want you to behave yourself, Luce…'

'What do you think I'm going to do, Mum?' Lucy asked sulkily. 'Stick a toad under his pillow? Put bubble bath in the loo? I'm not into *pranks*.'

It was just as well, Jessica thought one hour later as the car ate up the miles on the motorway, that Anthony was an accomplished conversationalist.

Co-operation from the back seat was conspicuous by its absence. Mark and Lucy sat and conversed in sporadic, huddled undertones. Clearly he had been as reluctant to come on the trip as Lucy had been, and Jessica could feel waves of hostility emanating from him. She was sure that Anthony could as well, but, if so, he gave little indication of it from his expression.

He had been quite charming from the start. The perfect gentleman, really, she told herself repeatedly. So what if they were going to be under the same roof for two days? Since when did a girl have anything to be wary of from a perfect gentleman?

She was surprised, though, at how much she had absorbed about him in how little time.

She'd answered the door, and his effect on her had been immediate—a highly sensitised awareness of that energy he gave off, that was apparent in the lean muscularity of his body and in the casual self-assurance of his bearing.

It was as hot as it had been for the past couple of weeks, and he was in a pair of khaki shorts. Long, sinewy legs were sprinkled with dark hair. Jessica had taken it all in with one glance, and had felt that strange stirring of something inside her, which she'd immediately stifled under her well honed, polite façade.

Thank heavens, in a way, for Lucy. Offhand, unimpressed by the car, barely communicative with Anthony beyond the absolute minimum. Still, her presence reminded Jessica of why she was sitting here now, speeding along to a country house somewhere far from the madding crowd. It also reminded her that she was a mother, a woman in her thirties who had left the world of girlish infatuation behind so long ago that she could barely remember having been there.

She was a parent, like Anthony. Two mature adults co-operating for the benefit of their respective children. She had no need to sparkle, or bewitch, or attract. Not, she thought, that she would be able to do any such things anyway.

But wasn't it reassuring not to feel any pressure to try?

She asked courteous, informed questions about where they were going, and spent most of the journey staring out of the window in apparent fascination at the scenery flashing past them. From the congested streets of London to the motorway, and finally off the motorway and down a series of roads that became more and more rural until the car headed away from the beaten track completely.

Occasionally she glanced across at him, at the long fingers idly curled around the gear shaft, the powerful arms, the easy elegance of his body.

She was aware of Lucy's voice chatting in a desultory fashion now and again from the back seat. By the sounds of it, she too felt little need to shine in the presence of Mark. There was no flushing coyness in her responses to him. Jessica wouldn't have been a bit surprised if she had looked around and seen her daughter nodding off. Lucy might not realise it, but Jessica could see, clearly enough, that her daughter's relationship with Mark had all the makings of a lifelong friendship—there was a touching camaraderie between them that included long periods of silence as perfectly acceptable.

She was reflecting on this, vaguely aware that they must be approaching their destination because the road could not possibly become much narrower, when Elmsden reared up in front of them.

Good heavens, she thought, for the past ten minutes they had been driving through his *estate*! Now they had rounded a corner, and there it was—gigantic, majestic, awe-inspiring. A house in name only. In reality, a mansion.

It wasn't simply the beauty of the design that struck Jessica, but the enormity of the place.

Before her parents' finances had taken a beating, she could remember, dimly, the large Victorian house they had lived in. She had been a child then, no more than eight or nine, and her memories were of a vast place. She realised now that it had been anything but vast. It had been minuscule compared to this edifice.

'Good Lord!' she heard herself exclaim.

Anthony turned to her and smiled. 'Meet Elmsden House,' he murmured. 'I assure you that only a part of it is maintained for use. It's been in the family for generations,' he explained, pulling up in the courtyard outside.

'You grew up here?' Jessica asked, looking at him. 'How on earth did you communicate with your parents? By remote control?'

'Ha, ha,' Lucy contributed from the back, opening her door. 'Mum's made a joke.' She grinned and sauntered outside, flexing her arms—supple, young and indifferent to her surroundings. 'Great spot for holding an open-air concert,' she said to no one in particular. 'Think of it—no one would have to drive back home!'

Mark, also outside the car now, laughed, and Anthony muttered under his breath, 'What a grim idea.'

'Lucy!' Jessica called, opening her door and standing with one foot out, breathing in the fresh, unpolluted air. 'Your bag?'

'Stan will bring them in,' Anthony said, as on cue the front door was opened, framing a man and a woman who were smiling and bustling forward.

But Lucy, naturally, said with aggravated politeness, 'I'm quite strong enough to carry my own bag.' She hoisted it over one shoulder, and she and Mark headed towards the house, heads bent towards each other, conversing about God only knew what.

Which left Jessica and Anthony.

'Shall I show Mrs…?' the woman, mid-fifties, rotund, kindly-faced, looked at Jessica questioningly '…to her room?'

'Jessica,' Jessica said, smiling and extending her hand. 'Jessica Hirst. I'm very glad to meet you both.'

The couple smiled in unison.

'I'll take her up, Maddie,' Anthony said. 'Which room have you prepared?'

'The green one for Mrs Hirst and the one next to it for her daughter.'

Green room? Were there so many guest bedrooms that they were colour coded?

When she was a child, her parents' house had had two guest bedrooms, and at the time that had been considered wildly extravagant. It had also had a large garden—unusual for a London property—and a conservatory, of all things. Jessica rarely remembered details of where she had spent the first few years of her life, but now, as they walked up to the front door, she recalled the feeling of *smallness* in that very first Victorian house. A child echoing in a big house.

She followed Anthony into the hall and experienced that feeling of smallness once more, of being dwarfed by the magnificence of her surroundings.

It was a vast hall, dominated and split in half by a winding staircase, and hung with paintings which were noble rather than pretty, and had clearly been handed down through the generations. Most were portraits, and

Jessica scanned them quickly to see whether she could spot a family resemblance anywhere.

'It's a beautiful house,' she said, looking around her, wondering whether 'house' was really an appropriate word. 'So large! You must have rattled around in it!'

'If I did, I never noticed at the time.' He followed her gaze politely, then began leading the way up the winding staircase. 'But then, there were always guests. A series of them. And parties on the weekends. My parents were always fond of the good life. I think they decided from a very early age that if they were going to live in the country, then they would make sure that isolation wasn't part of the package.' He spoke over his shoulder, glancing at her every now and then to make sure that she was still behind him.

Her parents had had friends too, she thought wistfully. Once. Before the big house had been sold and they had been forced to move down, ever down, into a series of smaller and smaller properties. Not too many friends left by then. A few stalwart ones, but even they, towards the end, had deserted the sinking ship. They'd been able to cope with the misfortune of her father's company collapsing, of the pressure of mounting debt. More difficult to cope with had been his steady decline into gambling and alcoholism.

It surprised her how much of her past she had put behind her. The mind, she supposed, always blocked out what it didn't want to see, and, really, what was the point of remembering the past when there was nothing you could do to alter the memories?

Had she ever known any real happiness?

She could remember the bickering, her father's belligerence after he had been at the bottle, her mother cowering in the background. She could remember hiding.

She seemed to have spent a great deal of her childhood hiding, but things couldn't have always been bad. There must have been a time when life had been easier.

Was that why she had been so susceptible to the outward charms of Eric Dean? Because he had been kind? A refuge in the storm when things had been particularly bad?

'Hello? Are you still here?'

Anthony's voice was right beside her, and she jumped.

'Oh! I was just wondering where Luce and Mark were,' she said, instinctively stepping away from him.

'Were you?' He looked down at her curiously, his eyes narrowed, and she had a feeling of being stripped of every outer layer, until her most private thoughts were exposed. 'You seemed very absorbed just then...'

'Which is my room? I wouldn't mind freshening up a bit.'

'Of course.' But he was well aware of her retreat, and he gave her another one of those cool, stripping glances before continuing up the stairs.

Her room was on the next landing. Along the way, they passed a door which opened into a small, well-stocked library, then a large sitting room, which seemed a very odd thing to have on a first floor. Next to that was Lucy's room. Jessica could see the unpacked overnight bag dumped on the bed. And opposite was her room, the green room—appropriately named because it had been decorated in various shades of green. Pale green carpet, cream and green striped wallpaper, cream and green flowered curtains and sofa, large four-poster bed with an elaborate bedspread that matched the curtains and the sofa.

'There's a bathroom just through that door,' Anthony

said, pointing to one corner of the room. 'And lunch will probably be outside.' He looked at his watch. 'In half an hour.'

'Right.' Jessica turned to look at him. He wasn't smiling. She could feel him *thinking*.

'You're an intensely private person, aren't you?' he remarked casually, not following her into the room, but lounging against the door frame, arms folded. There was nothing threatening about his question, but still she felt threatened. At any rate, her privacy did.

'Not unusually so, I don't think,' she replied neutrally.

'I'm slowly realising that I don't know a damn thing about you.' The grey eyes looked her over carefully, and again she felt that sensation of *speculations* being made. 'You have a daughter, you're unmarried, you work in a legal office somewhere in London.'

'What else is there to know?' Jessica asked with a nervous laugh.

'*What* made you decide to come and see me in the first place?'

'I thought you knew… I was worried about Lucy. I thought that your son might have been exerting some kind of influence over her.' She looked back at him warily.

'Why didn't you just wait and see whether she would settle down in time? Most parents accept small acts of rebellion as part and parcel of growing up.'

'Yes, I could have,' she answered evasively. Why was he asking her these questions? Why the sudden interest? It alarmed her because he struck her as the persevering type, not the sort to be fobbed off with a litany of pat responses.

'But you didn't, did you? That's precisely my point.'

'I really don't quite see what you're getting at…'

'I think you do,' he said smoothly. 'I think you see very well what I'm getting at. You just don't want to answer my questions, do you? Why? Why so reticent?'

'If I had known that this weekend would include answering questions about myself, then I wouldn't have accepted your invitation,' Jessica replied coldly. 'It was kind of you to think of us and ask us up here. I just hope you don't think that that gives you the right to try and pry into my personal life.'

'Is there one?' He raked her face. 'Or is Lucy your personal life?'

Jessica felt two spots of burning colour on her cheeks. 'That's hardly any of your business! I don't feel the need to ask *you* about your personal life, do I?'

'I get the feeling that you built a shell around yourself years ago, and you spend most of your time hiding inside it.'

She felt anger and confusion begin to spread through her like poison, until her hands were trembling and she had to hold them together to still them.

'Lucy is very important to me; I can't deny that. Single mothers can be very protective of their children, sometimes more so than married ones, because there's no partner for them to fall back on, to share concerns with.'

'Quite.' He straightened up and stuck his hands in his pockets. 'If there's anything else you need, please let me know. Maddie's usually very good at preparing the guest rooms. I'll see you by the swimming pool in a while.'

'Yes.' Relief. For a minute there her body had been rigid with apprehension. Most people backed off the minute she erected her defences. He was the first man who had dared to try and penetrate them, and it had rattled her; there was no denying that.

*   *   *

She had just finished showering when the bedroom door was pushed open, and her immediate and horrified reaction was to yank her dressing gown tightly around her.

It was only Lucy.

'Why have a shower when you can swim in the pool?' she asked, flinging herself on the bed and kicking off her shoes. 'That's how I shall be spending the afternoon, anyway.'

'Where have you been?'

'Exploring.' She propped herself up on her elbows and stared at her mother, who was now changing into a pair of shorts and a sleeveless shirt. 'The question is, what have *you* been doing?'

'Oh, not this again, Luce.'

'What?'

'Don't put on that innocent look. I can see right through it.'

'You're red. Have I struck a raw nerve? Have you been getting up to anything with the master of the house?' She grinned and sat up, cross-legged, on the bed. 'I think you should, Mum. No point remaining a spinster for the rest of your life! Even if you don't get married, you could at least go out there and have a bit of fun.'

'Lucy!'

'Well…you're from that hippie generation of peace and love and all that, aren't you?'

'It was a bit before my time, actually.'

'Well, I still think that you should get out there and test the water.'

'Thank you for your advice. I hope you haven't been following it yourself, *miss*.' It was a clever ploy, turning the tables. In the mirror, she could see her daughter's face redden.

'Just the other day you were lecturing me about boy-friends!'

'Are you sleeping with anyone?'

'Really! Mum!' Not a denial, but there was enough horror in the voice for Jessica to know that Lucy had not yet begun those games, and she inwardly breathed a sigh of relief. 'I'm going to change into my swimming costume,' Lucy said, heaving herself off the bed, 'if staying here means having to answer a bunch of nosy questions.'

'Lunch is outside,' Jessica said mildly. 'I'm not sure where; probably by the swimming pool. In fifteen minutes. Please do the polite thing and show up on time.'

'I might,' Lucy informed her airily, heading out of the room. 'I might not.'

But, thankfully, she was there when Jessica finally found her way to the pool twenty minutes later.

Maddie had laid the table outside with a spread of cold food. Mark and Lucy had obviously partaken of some, and were now in the swimming pool. Anthony, sitting under the umbrella with just his swimming trunks on, looked at her as she approached.

'Aren't you going to have a dip?' he asked, as soon as she sat down.

'I forgot to bring my costume.' Thank heavens. It was distracting enough having to look at this man in just his bathing trunks, without the embarrassment of semi-nudity on her part as well.

Why was she so aware of him? She commented politely on the food, slipped on a pair of sunglasses, sipped some of the fresh lemonade and tried not to notice the sheer perfection of his body. His stomach was flat, hard, with dark hair spiralling out of sight beneath the waist-band of the trunks.

Jessica felt her imagination begin to fly, and stoutly anchored it firmly back on terra firma.

They conversed, but sporadically. The sun made her sluggish, and the conversation was frequently interrupted by Lucy and Mark emerging from the pool at regular intervals to eat. They both seemed to eat like horses, devouring food with the rapidity of people emerging from a starvation diet.

'Your mother tells me that she hasn't brought a swim-ming costume,' Anthony said, catching Lucy before she could vanish back into the pool.

Maddie was clearing the dishes away, replacing the jug of lemonade with another.

'Oh, Mum! And after you nagged me into bringing mine! Aren't you boiling?'

'I'm absolutely fine, darling.'

'No, you're not. You're boiling. I can tell. You're as red as a berry.'

Jessica smiled and wondered whether she could get away with strangling her daughter on the spot.

'Have you put on any sun block?' she asked, and Lucy shook her head.

'Nope. I'm only going to be here for a little while longer, anyway. Mark's going to take me into Stratford.'

'Does he know that?' Jessica looked at the figure in the pool, floating and seemingly asleep on a large, in-flatable tyre.

'Oh, yes.' Lucy gulped down some more lemonade enthusiastically. 'When I'm ready, I shall just tip him off that tyre.'

'Typical woman,' Anthony teased. 'Forever using force to get her own way.'

'Actually,' Lucy informed him, 'I hate men who generalise about women.'

'Sorry. Accept my humble apologies.'

Jessica hid a smile and stared out at the pool and the indolent figure in it.

'Haven't you got a costume that Mum could borrow?' Lucy asked, ignoring the apology and also ignoring the expression on her mother's face at this suggestion. 'This house is so big; there must be a spare swimsuit lurking somewhere in one of the bedrooms.'

'There should be, now that you mention it. Fiona uses the pool whenever she can. I'm pretty sure she would have left a swimsuit or two lying around.'

'I really couldn't...' Jessica said hastily, glaring at Lucy.

'Why not? Who's Fiona?'

'Fiona is—'

'An occasional guest here,' Anthony interrupted. He turned and looked at Jessica, squinting as the sun caught his eyes. 'She usually uses the room you're in. Have a look in one of the drawers. You should find something there.'

'We're differently built,' Jessica said flatly. 'I very much doubt that any of her swimsuits would fit.'

'Well, Mum, you could always swim *au naturel*.' Lucy grinned cheerfully at this suggestion. 'It's pretty private here. Oh, apart from you,' she added, glancing at Anthony and idly picking ice cubes out of her glass and eating them. 'But you wouldn't mind, would you?'

Jessica wondered whether parents could divorce their children.

'Not at all.' He shrugged and glanced at Jessica. 'I don't think she'd agree to that suggestion, though, do you?'

'No, Mum can be a bit reserved like that.'

'Would you two mind not talking about me as though I wasn't here?' she said, snapping out of sheer embarrassment. 'Lucy, *go away*!'

'Oh, charming! One minute you're telling me that I can't go anywhere, and the next minute you're yelling at me to go away! I can't win! I'll only go if you put on one of Fiona's swimsuits. There's no point you sitting there frying in the sun like a lobster.'

'Lobsters don't *fry in the sun*,' Jessica told her, just managing not to snarl.

'You're cross. I can tell. You're being pedantic.'

'Children!' Jessica muttered under her breath, standing up. 'All right, I'll go and try on one of those wretched swimsuits.'

'I'll come with you.'

'No need.'

'Just to make sure that you don't lock yourself in the bedroom and hide.' She turned to Anthony with a shrug. 'Such a child sometimes.'

Jessica grabbed her daughter by the elbow. That's it, she thought. If this is Lucy in high spirits, then she'd better fly back down to earth. Heaven only knows *what* she'll be saying next if she doesn't.

CHAPTER SIX

'I LOOK ridiculous.' There had been six swimsuits in the chest of drawers in the bedroom, which had made Jessica wonder whether Fiona did anything other than sunbathe during her trips to Elmsden House. Apparently not.

And, inevitably as far as she was concerned, they were all bikinis.

The choice rested not so much on which was the most flattering colour, but which was the least minuscule. It had been a difficult choice. Jessica couldn't remember having ever seen such skimpy swimwear outside a magazine. Certainly, she had never owned anything along these lines herself. Nor in such quantity. Two one-pieces in sober colours had been her concession to the sunbathing industry over the years.

What had ever been the point of investing in any more? She had yet to go abroad to a sunny country for a holiday, and the weather in England was simply too unreliable in summer to warrant spending hard-earned cash on items of clothing that would spend most of their time at the bottom of a drawer.

'I've seen worse,' Lucy said, with disheartening candour. 'You have a couple of stretchmarks on your stomach, that's all.'

'Thanks very much, Luce. Any more compliments where those came from?' She eyed herself critically in the mirror. A couple of stretchmarks? Trust Lucy to zoom in on what she herself had quite happily chosen to miss for the past sixteen-odd years.

She grabbed a towel from the bathroom, feeling increasingly nervous as they made their way back to the swimming pool. In the interim, Lucy, speaking from the Olympian heights of teenage suppleness, had proceeded to mention why her mother should think about taking up some regular form of exercise. Anyone would think, Jessica said tartly, that she was in the running for the fat lady at the Circus, which provoked the expected round of laughter.

It would be pointless to wish that Anthony had vanished from the poolside area, perhaps to take an important overseas call which would helpfully last for a couple of hours, but she went ahead and wished it anyway.

When was the last time she had felt so nervous about how she looked?

It had been bad enough squeezing into a bikini that was really a size too small for her, particularly in the bust area, and Lucy's frank and open observations had hardly helped matters.

At least, though, she wasn't sniping and whinging. There had been little or no mention of the 'event of the century' rock concert which she was missing, and no sulks at all.

Jessica made a deliberate effort to smile broadly at the thought of that as they meandered out towards the pool.

Predictably, Lucy plunged into the water as soon as they were there, and even more predictably Anthony looked up from where he was sitting, still in the same spot under the umbrella by the table, and stared at her as she approached.

'Found something, I see.'

'Found several things,' Jessica replied, unable to sustain the stare and looking away towards the pool. 'Of which this was the least...the least outrageous.'

'Fiona does like to parade,' Anthony said, and at the thought of the other woman waltzing up and down by a turquoise swimming pool, clad in six inches of stretchy fabric, Jessica felt a swift stab of envy.

At that age, she thought, I was busy bringing up baby, trying to juggle my life so that I could be a mother and earn some money at the same time.

No mother, even, to help her find her feet in a new and scary world.

Despite her father's drinking problems, it had ironically been her mother who had been the first to go, and after that, well, she might just as well have become even more invisible than she already had been. Her father had thrown himself into yet more drink with frightening desperation. He'd barely acknowledged her presence in the house at all.

She had always accepted that it could have been a lot worse. He could have become physically abusive. As it was, she'd merely had the sad and dubious privilege of having complete, utter and lonely privacy at the age of fifteen and a half. She'd been able to come and go as she liked, see just whosoever she wanted. She could have jumped off a cliff, for that matter. Her father would never have noticed.

'You're doing it again,' Anthony said, and she literally jumped and refocused her eyes on him.

'Doing what?'

'Drifting off into some other world of your own.'

'And you're doing it again as well,' Jessica said brusquely.

'What?'

'Trying to speculate on my private life.'

She could not make out his expression behind his sunglasses, but she didn't have to. It was apparent in the thinning of his mouth.

Jessica sat back with a mental shrug and watched as her daughter emerged, dripping, from the pool, followed by Mark. They were laughing, a sound which had been all too unfamiliar over the past few months, and Jessica automatically smiled, looking at them.

'We're off,' Lucy announced, slinging a towel around herself and squeezing her hair between her hands.

'Off? Where to?' It dawned on her that she would be left alone with Anthony, and, much as she tried to approach this in an adult way, she still felt a sudden, panicky trepidation at the prospect.

'Stratford,' Lucy explained in a long-suffering, exaggeratedly patient voice. She had cultivated this little trait and honed it down to a fine art so that it never failed to get on Jessica's nerves.

'We're going to indulge in a spot of culture,' Mark said, not looking at his father at all and concentrating all his attention on Jessica. 'Do all the touristy things like look around Will Shakespeare's house. Fascinating from an artistic point of view, apart from anything else.'

At which Anthony snorted and glared at his son in disgust.

'That sounds like fun,' Jessica said hurriedly. 'What time can we expect you back?'

'Here we go again,' Lucy said, scowling. 'Mum and her fanatical clock-watching.'

'Oh, we should only be a couple of hours,' Mark said, walking off while Lucy followed.

'Going to have a look around Will Shakespeare's house,' Anthony said, as soon as they were out of earshot. He took off his sunglasses and rubbed his eyes with his fingers. 'Sees nothing wrong with that, but if I asked him to come and have a look around the company he'd run a mile.'

Jessica tilted her head back so that it was resting comfortably half off the back of the patio chair and didn't say anything. Every time father and son were together, there was an electric current of unease running between them, and she had already decided that she would ignore any such tension. It was enough coping with her own daughter's mood swings.

'Consider yourself lucky that you have a daughter who's got her head screwed on.'

At this, Jessica twisted slightly so that she was looking at him. It was an awkward angle—something she only realised afterwards. The swimsuit top had been fashioned for someone flatter chested. Now, out of the corner of her eye, she could see the cloth virtually only managing to cover her nipple, and she rearranged herself accordingly.

Anthony Newman wasn't looking at her. At least not in any way that could possibly suggest anything sexual. He wasn't really even seeing her. His forehead was creased in a dark frown—he was thinking of his son, that much was obvious. So why did she still feel so hotly aware of him? So desperate to make sure that she maintained a façade of cool aplomb?

'What do you mean, "got her head screwed on"?'

'Planning on doing something useful with her life.'

'And that's your definition of happiness? Doing something useful with one's life?'

'Isn't it yours?' He narrowed his eyes and regarded her coolly.

'No, of course it's not!'

'Then why on earth are you so concerned with whether Lucy goes on to university or not?'

It was an obvious question, but it still left her feeling as though she had been wrong-footed. She took a deep breath to keep her temper in check.

'It wouldn't bother me whether Lucy wanted to study art or economics,' she said evenly. 'Just so long as she was happy.'

'Progressing her education.'

'Presumably you want Mark to progress his as well?' Jessica asked sweetly.

'It would help if he could progress it in a slightly more useful manner.' He raked his fingers through his hair, and she felt a sudden, unexpected burst of sympathy. It must be hard, she supposed, to be at the very top of business and finance and to know that your son had little or no interest in the world you'd taken pains to build.

What had happened to his wife?

It wasn't the first time she had asked herself that question. Every time, her speculations on the subject became slightly more detailed.

'It would help if you gave him a bit more support, I suppose,' she said, matter-of-factly.

'And how would you advise me to do that?' Anthony growled. 'Take time off to tour a few art galleries?'

'That mightn't be a bad idea! Have you ever been inside an art gallery?'

'Naturally! I'm not completely uncultured. Believe it or not, though, I rarely have time to indulge in such leisurely pursuits.'

You have enough time to indulge in leisurely pursuits with the owner of this bikini, though, Jessica thought. She remembered what her initial impression of Anthony Newman had been, even before she had met him—that he was a workaholic, too preoccupied for the needs of his son. The situation, she acknowledged, might not be quite as clear-cut as she had originally assumed, but in a nutshell wasn't that the problem?

She looked at him and realised that her anger stemmed only in part from this. Most of it stemmed from the image of him with Fiona.

'You could make time,' she heard herself tell him. 'It would probably do your son a world of good to know that you're not entirely against the idea of him studying art at university.'

'Oh, but I am,' Anthony said silkily.

'Why?'

'Because—' He stopped short and threw her a dark, exasperated glance.

'Because…?'

'Because his mother was an artist,' Anthony told her, his voice hard. 'She spent quite a lot of time waffling on about the importance of being creative. What she really meant was the importance of self-gratification.'

'What happened to her?' She realised that she was holding her breath, that her heart was thumping in her chest.

'She was involved in an accident when Mark was two. The small aircraft she was in went down in poor weather conditions.'

'I'm very sorry. Poor Mark.'

'Poor Mark has had a life full of everything money can buy.'

'Oh, well, in that case, what a lucky child!' she said sarcastically, and she was gratified to see his face darken with colour.

'You should be a teacher,' he said under his breath. 'You certainly have a way of psychologically rapping over the knuckles.'

Jessica felt her eyes sting at that, even though it was

hardly an outright insult. Some might even construe it as a backhanded compliment of sorts, but she didn't. Recently, her self-confidence had been too precarious for her to nod enthusiastically at the remark.

Her running arguments with Lucy had forced her into the role of harpy, and his observation only seemed to confirm the opinion.

'I'm going for a swim,' she muttered, and before he could answer she walked towards the pool and slipped in, swimming under water for the length of it, and wishing that she could just carry on like that indefinitely.

It was cold, but not unpleasant. She got to the end of the pool, gasped as she breathed in a lungful of air, and then dived back under, swimming blindly, eyes closed against the chlorine and against her disproportionate reaction to his stupid, unfair remark.

She crashed into him without warning and rose, spluttering to the surface.

'I apologise if I upset you,' he said, which made her even angrier with him and with herself.

'Forget it!' She prepared to turn away and head back for the deep end, but he caught her by the shoulders and turned her to face him.

'You're quite probably right. I should be more enthusiastic about Mark, or at least do him the favour of feigning enthusiasm, but it's a damn hard world out there, and painting pictures isn't going to get him very far.'

'You make it sound so trivial—"painting pictures". Besides, I don't think you have the faintest idea what your son intends to do. I don't think he wants to pursue any kind of career in fine art. I think he's more interested in commercial art, or graphic art.' Yes, she was talking absolute sense. Yes, her mouth was doing precisely what it should be doing—giving voice to rational thought.

Everything else, though, was being churned up in some weird blender. She was so close to him that she could hardly breathe, for a start, and her skin was prickling all over. If she moved a muscle, she knew that she would somehow make a complete fool of herself.

'Where's the difference?' he asked softly. His hands moved to cup her face, and really she didn't know what to do. She knew what she *should* do. She *should* move away, firmly but politely, so that he was aware that he was invading her private space, but how could she do that when her limbs could hardly move?

'The difference...' she began bravely, but his eyes were boring into her. 'Could we have this conversation somewhere else...?' she finished lamely.

'Where do you have in mind?'

Was he flirting? Just the possibility of it threw her into a state of renewed confusion.

'I'm beginning to get cold.'

He turned away and headed out of the pool, and, heart thumping, Jessica followed.

No, he wasn't flirting. That was her imagination playing tricks on her. Hardly surprising, was it? She had spent the past sixteen-odd years in an emotional and physical deep-freeze; her first and last experience with a man had been a disaster. Was it any wonder that Anthony Newman was having this effect on her? He was terrifyingly attractive, after all. And that way he had of looking, of talking... Well, it would go to any girl's head, especially a girl who hadn't known the feeling since she had been a teenager.

She sat at a distance from him and made herself concentrate on Fiona. And on Eric. A combination of the two would rescue her from the foolish, drowning sensation she had every time he looked at her.

'I really don't think that Mark intends to while away his time locked up in an attic somewhere painting pictures, as you call it. And, even if he did, why on earth shouldn't you support him?'

'I think we've covered this one already.' He leaned back, arms loosely linked behind his head, and closed his eyes.

It was infuriating. How could someone who was so obviously astute when it came to his dealings with other people fail to see what was as plain as the nose on his face? That his son needed him?

'It would be a very boring place if we all tried to become company directors.'

'I agree. Painting pictures is fine for anyone else.'

'But not for your son.'

He turned and looked at her coolly and without flinching. 'I don't think that you can exactly lecture me on the subject.'

'Meaning…?'

'Meaning that leaving school is presumably fine, as far as you're concerned, for anyone else. But not for your daughter.'

'That's not at all what I mean!' Jessica glared at him crossly.

'You're so terrified at the thought that she might not want to go to university, that she might not want to forge a career for herself, that you'd lock her away in a tower until her exams were over.'

'That's ridiculous!' Jessica muttered uncomfortably. She stuck on her sunglasses and resolutely looked away.

'You're as guilty of trying to live your life through your daughter as you claim that I am through my son.'

'I just want what's best for her.'

'You just want what's best for yourself.'

She found that she was clenching the arms of the chair. It was a good thing that they weren't made of glass. They would have splintered into a thousand pieces.

'You,' she said fiercely, 'are the most...*aggravating* man I have ever, *ever* met in my life. Do you know what it's like...? No, of course you don't.' She could hear the unpleasant note of bitterness creeping into her voice, her past catching up with her and tripping her up.

He moved swiftly. It didn't help that she had refocused her gaze mutinously on the pool. If she had been looking at him, seen him coming towards her, she would have taken defensive measures. As it was, one minute he was in his chair, the next minute he was in front of her, leaning over her, his hands on either side of her chair.

'Do I know what *what*'s like?' he asked. 'And take these damned things off. I want to see your eyes when you're talking to me.' He reached and pulled off her sunglasses, and without them she felt horribly unprotected, like a fish out of water gasping in the air.

'Nothing!'

'You imagine that I don't have the same sort of ambition for Mark as you have for Lucy simply because he has a cushion of money to fall back on.'

'That's not what I meant at all.'

'Of course it is.'

The atmosphere between them was so thick that she felt as if she could reach out and cup a handful of it.

'You have to admit that he *is* protected.'

'I admit nothing of the sort. In some respects it's worse, because he has to fight his way out of wealth. He has to learn how to stand on his own two feet and make his own mark in life without assuming that he can depend on me to bail him out whenever he needs it.'

'You just don't understand,' Jessica muttered stubbornly. She didn't dare look at him. She dreaded that he might read the undercurrent of awareness lying beneath the anger.

He reached out and grasped her hair in his fingers, brushing the side of her face, drawing her to face him.

'I find you as aggravating as you find me,' he said in a barely audible voice. 'And I understand more than you think. You're desperate for your daughter not to fall into the same trap as you think you've fallen into—but you can't go on protecting her for ever, and you certainly can't go on living your life through her.'

'That's third-rate psychoanalysis, Anthony Newman, and you know it.'

'It's third-rate psychoanalysis because you don't happen to agree with it.'

That, she thought resentfully, made her sound narrow-minded and she wasn't narrow-minded. She knew that. In fact, she had always made a point of adopting a liberal, 'live and let live' view about things, about life in general. She stood on the sidelines and was quite content to let the rest of the human race get on with doing whatever they saw fit to do.

Except, she thought uncomfortably, when she reasoned things out that way, she hardly came out any better, did she? Perhaps not narrow-minded, but, in a way, worse—she saw herself as uninvolved with the whole business of living, just concerned with the business of existing.

Had Eric done that to her? Had he shut her away? She had never thought about it before, but now she wondered how much she could continue to blame that brief, disastrous relationship for the rest of her life.

Anthony Newman made her ask these questions, she thought suddenly; he kept shoving his little insights down her throat. Couldn't he see that she was much happier paddling about undisturbed in her little murky pond?

'Think what you want, then,' she muttered, with a stubborn refusal to enter into the conversation.

'Why, for instance, isn't there a man in your life now, if not because you want to protect Lucy from what you would see as an intruder? An intruder into the little world you've concocted for yourself and your daughter?'

'That's utterly unfair!' She shot him an angry look.

'Is it?'

'You don't know what you're talking about!' And anyway, she thought, you're a fine one to launch into a monologue on someone else's faults. It was hardly as though he could be entered for the Father of the Year contest.

'Would you admit it if I did?'

Jessica stared at him in mute silence. No, she thought, she wouldn't. And why should she? It was her life, wasn't it? She could lead it any way she wanted to, and she wasn't accountable to anyone for her decision.

Not that long ago, she would have been proud of that stance, would have seen it as the spirit of independence.

She wondered—and the thought skimmed the surface of her mind so fleetingly that it was gone before she could capture it—whether she hadn't rooted herself in independence after all, but in an isolation that would come back to haunt her.

Lucy wouldn't be around for ever. Those days of being physically needed were over. The nest was being vacated, and then what?

She felt a chill wind blow over her.

'You're damned stubborn,' he murmured, but his tone had altered, become softer, less accusatory.

'If you say so.'

'Yes, I do. And it's very childish to take refuge behind sulks.'

'I'm not sulking.'

'Not that you don't look quite captivating with that pout.'

Had she been pouting? She tried not to now; she tried to rearrange her features into some semblance of calm, sensible maturity. I'm still damned furious with you, she thought. I still resent it that you feel you have the right to lecture me on my abilities as a mother, even if some of what you say is true.

But when she looked down all she could see were his hands, gripping the sides of the chair, the sprinkling of dark hair on his arms. When she breathed, she breathed in the aroma of his maleness, and it was like incense. Powerful, disorientating.

'I think I'll go in now,' she said, shuffling in the chair but not moving too much because she didn't want to physically touch him. What if she got burnt? She had the strangest feeling that she might.

'Already?'

'It's very hot out here.'

'And you're furious with me for barging into your privacy.'

Jessica tried to ignore the effect he was having on her by recapturing some of the anger she had felt only minutes before.

'Let's just say that we agree to differ. I'm a guest

here,' she said, looking up at him and catching his eyes full on. 'So I'm not prepared to launch into some kind of counter-attack on you.'

Now that she was looking at him, she couldn't unfasten her eyes from his face. It was like being hypnotised. Her mouth parted, though not because she had anything further to add on the subject, but simply because her mind was so fuddled that she no longer seemed to have the will-power to direct her thoughts.

And she knew, before he kissed her, exactly what he was going to do. She could read the subliminal message in his eyes, though she would have sworn that the feeling took him as much by surprise as it did her.

He lowered his head, and his mouth was on hers, the persuasive feel of lips against hers, his tongue meeting hers.

Jessica moaned weakly as the intensity of the kiss deepened, pushing her against the chair, forcing her head back so that her hair hung over the back of it.

The heat from the sun on her body was nothing compared to the molten heat raging inside her. She didn't pull his head towards her, but neither did she push him away.

It was the first time she had been kissed in years. Oh, she had had the odd peck on the mouth at Christmas parties, by a work colleague. She had had a casual embrace and had willingly returned it in the same casual, friendly spirit in which it had been given.

But nothing like this. She didn't think that she had *ever* been kissed like this before. She felt as though she was losing touch with reality. His mouth left hers to trail hungrily along her cheekbones and along her neck, and Jessica closed her eyes. She could barely breathe properly. It was more a case of panting rather than breathing, and his breathing was uneven as well, as though he had initiated something that had caught him as unawares as it had caught her.

He caught her hair in his hands, tilting her head to accommodate his exploring mouth, which found the sensitive spot behind her ear. He licked it. He blew into it, and she groaned and twisted against him.

Her breasts ached. She wanted him to touch them. Her body felt so good with what he was doing to it that she could hardly believe herself to be the same woman who had felt no stirrings of temptation at all over the countless, untouched years.

It was completely noiseless by the pool. A slight breeze half-heartedly rustled the leaves on the trees and the bushes bordering the patio. In contrast, every sound they made seemed to be amplified a thousand times. Her own breathing was deafening, and her tiny moans seemed crashingly exaggerated against the silence.

His hands left her hair and one finger now moved in a light, stroking motion along her cleavage, then along the outside of the bikini top, up along the fine straps, then back down to her cleavage, and over the top of the material so that it circled her breasts, touching the nipple which hardened in excitement.

Jessica arched back a little further, hardly daring to breathe as he lifted both straps of the bikini down.

With one teenaged daughter and a life which she had always thought had inured her against surprises, she was stunned to find herself feeling like a virgin. But, of course, in a way, she very nearly was, wasn't she? Lucy was the product of fifteen minutes with Eric Dean, and after him there had been no one. Her body, asleep for years, was being awakened and was responding with all the savage, frightening force of a woman being touched for the first time.

He didn't try to unclasp the back of the bathing-suit top. Instead he eased it down over her breasts, and although she wasn't looking at him she was aware that he was no longer bending over her, but somehow kneeling in front of her so that his head was on a level with her breasts.

He took them in his hands, and Jessica lay back with a soaring feeling of complete desire. It washed over her in a wave, soaking every part of her body, moistening between her thighs.

Her nipples were erect and throbbing and it was sweet release when his tongue circled one, lapping against the hard, projecting bud, then his mouth closed over it, and for the first time she coiled her fingers in his hair and pushed his mouth ever harder against her. Wild craving surged through her, making her dizzy. She wanted him to continue sucking her breasts for ever; the feeling seemed just too good to stop.

While his mouth devoured her breasts, his hands found the waistband of the bikini, and he eased it down without removing it, pulling it low enough to part her legs, and Jessica slid a little down the chair. She no longer had to think about what she was doing. Her body was running on automatic now, doing what needed to be done to satisfy this suffocating need inside her.

He caressed the inside of her thighs, then she felt a warm breeze blow against her breasts, and he transferred his attentions to her stomach, lower and lower, until his tongue was moving between her legs, arousing her in a way she had never before experienced. She squirmed against his mouth, and as he explored deeper within her she felt her muscles tense and everything seemed to explode in a wonderful release.

With release came awareness, and with awareness came a wave of embarrassment. Jessica half opened her eyes and they looked at one another in silence.

She didn't have to say a word, though, because there was the sound of a car, and she sprang into frenzied action. From a mind drained of all thought, she now possessed a mind so full of thoughts that she couldn't move quickly enough.

'Oh, my God,' she said, standing up and getting herself into some kind of order.

'Calm down!'

Anthony grasped her forearms, and she hissed fiercely, 'Let me go! What was I *thinking* of? I must have been mad!'

'Why?'

'I don't want to discuss this!' And she really didn't. Even if Lucy weren't about to appear on the scene, she still would not have wanted to discuss it. In a way, she could thank her daughter because she knew well enough what would have happened if they hadn't been disturbed. There would have been nothing to pull her back from the brink. Mad, mad, mad!

She raked her fingers through her hair and walked unsteadily towards the side of the pool just as Lucy bounded onto the patio, the usual noise preceding her appearance.

Jessica swung around and pretended to be surprised. Out of the corner of her eye, she could see Anthony back in his chair, as cool and collected as though nothing had happened.

'Luce! You're back...early!'

'Don't tell me you haven't been in the water yet?'

Lucy said, ignoring Anthony completely and heading towards her mother. 'What on earth have you been doing for the past hour? Soaking up the sun? You'll get skin cancer. Especially with your complexion.'

'Where's Mark?'

'In the car. We got to Stratford to find that I'd forgotten my bag. Not that it's bulging with cash, but I couldn't bear to walk around without it so we came back. You're bursting out of that bikini, Mum. You need to go on a diet.' She swung around airily and winked in an obvious manner. 'Now, don't you two oldies get up to anything!' she said, which made Jessica want to find a nearby hole and scurry down it. When would her daughter ever learn the meaning of *tact*? *Diplomacy?*

'Be back in time for tea.'

'*Tea* is what children have at five-thirty, Mum. Fish fingers and baked beans. In these parts of the world—' she shot her mother a wicked grin '—it's served at eight and called *dinner*. With which she gave a shout of laughter, and Jessica, glaring and red-faced, dived cleanly into the pool.

CHAPTER SEVEN

JESSICA ignored Anthony when she finally emerged from the pool. She would have stayed there for ever, but Lucy had been right—she was prone to sunburn if she wasn't careful, and swimming in blazing sunshine for hours on end would have sent her into bed with raw red skin.

He looked at her without saying anything as she stepped out of the water and wrapped herself in her towel. And she was at a loss for words. Events kept replaying themselves in her head. Of their own accord. To look at him would be to reinforce the images, but to ignore him would be to give importance to what had taken place between them, and it hadn't been important.

I've been reckless, she told herself, I've acted out of character. Maybe years of enforced celibacy are finally coming to a head, but then that could be explained away. Lucy was growing up, if not grown up already. Subconsciously, Jessica concluded, she was beginning to re-establish the need for a life of her own, and coincidentally—unfortunate coincidence that it was—Anthony Newman happened to be around just when this mental reawakening was taking place.

He was attractive, charismatic, and perhaps his total unsuitability even went some way to giving him added appeal.

She sneaked a quick glance at him and he said, without inflection in his voice, 'Shall we just ignore what happened between us?'

Jessica shrugged and looked away, collecting her belongings and making a great performance of it as well.

'These things happen. The change of scenery, the weather…it's not important. I mean, it doesn't mean anything. I'm going upstairs for a rest. What time do you expect me to be down for supper?'

'Around seven-thirty.'

'Right. See you then.' She walked away, hoping that her air of self-confidence wouldn't be ambushed by an inability to find her way back to her bedroom. She would, she knew, rather have wandered lost in the place for a fortnight than retrace her footsteps to the pool so that she could ask for directions.

But she had no trouble in getting to her bedroom, where, away from the cool inspection of his eyes, she could relax and think about what had happened.

What *had* happened? Logic could explain away some of it, but where was *logic* when she needed it? She had led a restrained, reasonable life. She had learnt from bitter experience. Eric Dean had taken her innocence and girlish infatuation and used them against her, and she had resolved never to let anyone hurt her like that again.

So she had kept away from men. If she didn't get involved with them, then how on earth could she be hurt? It had always made sense.

So how was it that Anthony Newman had been able to infiltrate her layers of self-protection?

Of all people, Anthony Newman, she realised, might well be the most magnetic, but he was, likewise, the least reliable.

She stripped off and spent twenty-five minutes under the shower, washing him out of her mind—or at least attempting to.

When she stepped out of the shower and saw the bikini innocently hanging by the sink to dry, she remembered Fiona, and gave a start of dismay.

Only now had the other woman crossed her mind.

She wrapped the towel around her and stared at her reflection in the mirror.

What's happened to my conscience? she wondered. All this time thinking about myself, trying to work out what all this means in connection with me, but what about Fiona?

'You poor child,' she said to the mirror, but not so loudly that she felt a complete fool. This was quickly followed up by, 'You sod,' when she thought of Anthony and his complete lack of scruples. 'You make a habit of this, do you?' She reverted to speaking her thoughts to herself. You go around seducing every woman you happen to meet, regardless of whether you're committed to one already or not, do you? The thought of that made her sick.

This was worse than her experience with Eric. Worse because she was older, wiser and presumably capable of knowing which paths to tread and which to avoid. Worse because Anthony was far more lethal than Eric could ever aspire to be. Poor Eric, in retrospect, had been nothing but a pathetic con man, the sort of man who really can only deceive someone as young and as naive as she had been. Whereas Anthony— Well, he had all the dangers of the inveterate charmer. His intelligence, his self-assurance, his powerful good looks, were all the more potent because they were not feigned. Every quality in him was inbred. Therein lay the danger.

When she stepped out of the bathroom, she didn't at first see him because she had not been expecting to. In fact, she didn't look in the direction of the bed at all, and she only realised that he was sitting in the armchair next to it when she sat down at the dressing table, glanced in the mirror and saw him in the reflection.

Seeing a ghost would have given her less of a shock.

'What are you doing here?' she demanded, spinning around in the chair and dragging the towel tightly around her. 'What the *hell* are you doing here?' There was an edge of shrill panic in her voice which she made no effort to conceal.

'I did knock, but you didn't answer.'

'I was in the shower! Do you think I've got bionic hearing?' She looked at him, acutely aware of her state of semi-undress. 'Now, do you mind getting out of this room? Or do you make it a habit to barge in on your female guests whenever it suits you, simply because you own the house they're staying in?'

'I do not make it a habit to do anything of the sort,' he ground out. 'And, yes, I do mind getting out of this room. We need to talk about what happened, and talk we shall, whether you like it or not.'

'I have no intention of having a conversation with you…here…here in a bedroom, with me…like this!' She stood up, still clutching the towel, and walked towards the door purposefully. Her legs, at least, appeared to be doing all right, which was more than could be said for the rest of her body.

And what if Lucy returned back unexpectedly, and pranced into the bedroom to find them? Her daughter had a blind spot when it came to doors—she never seemed to knock on them. Jessica felt faint at the mere thought of it.

Anthony walked towards her without saying a word, but, instead of leaving, he leant against the door, arms folded, and regarded her in silence.

'I realise you want to pretend that nothing happened between us…'

'I don't want to do anything of the sort!' Jessica answered quickly, refusing to step back and show just how terrified she was of her body betraying her again. She desperately wished that she had had the good sense to lock her bedroom door, but the thought that he might enter unexpectedly had been the furthest thing from her mind at the time.

'What are you so afraid of?'

'I'm not afraid of anything!'

'You can relax. I have no intention of taking advantage of you, but I do think that we need to talk about what happened. I don't want you to leave here with all this bottled up inside of you. Worse, under the misapprehension that what happened was somehow all my fault.'

'I never said that it was your fault,' Jessica told him quickly. 'Just the opposite. Okay? Like I said, things happen unexpectedly; that's life.'

'But you don't speak from experience.'

Jessica looked at him, willing him to leave her alone to get on with her thoughts and to sort things out internally. She wasn't accustomed to pouring her feelings out to anyone. Circumstance had trained her to deal with her problems on her own. She had dealt with Eric on her own, she had dealt with her pregnancy on her own, and she had dealt with bringing up her daughter on her own. She could, she thought resentfully, take care of herself. She certainly didn't need Anthony Newman trying to wheedle confidences out of her.

'At the pool…'

'At the pool, I lost control.'

'And that terrifies you, doesn't it?'

'Doesn't it you?' She looked at him steadily, aware that she had to meet his eyes, keep him focused on looking at her face. If his eyes started drifting towards the rest of her body, she knew that she would feel even more vulnerable than she already did. 'You're in charge of a big company. You presumably bark out orders, take decisions, make targets. Are you telling me that you go around happily willing to let events dictate what you do with your life?' She gave a short laugh. 'If you don't mind me saying so, you strike me as the last person in the world to lecture on the advantages of losing control.'

'There's control at work and control in one's private life. The two don't even breathe the same atmosphere.'

'Could we finish this discussion some other time?' Jessica asked politely. 'Fascinating though it might be,' she added sarcastically, and he frowned with impatience.

'Sexual attraction has nothing to do with control,' he told her, his grey eyes lazily raking over her body.

Sexual attraction. Why was it that those two little words seemed so extraordinarily seductive when they came out of his lips? The last man who had shown an interest in her, who had told her that he was attracted to her, had almost made her laugh. She didn't feel like laughing now.

And sexual attraction, she wanted to tell him, *could* be controlled. Wasn't that what separated man from beast? The ability to control their responses?

'I'm not interested in playing games with you,' Jessica said coldly, to mask the heat that was treacherously surging through her. 'No doubt that's the kind of lifestyle that you lead. Brief affairs with obliging women.'

His lips thinned. 'You have an amazing capacity to jump to conclusions, do you know that? You did it when you assumed that Mark was some sort of subversive influence over your daughter before you'd even met him, and you're doing it now.'

Jessica felt her cheeks burn at this, but she didn't say a word. She just continued to watch him warily from under her lashes.

'Go away,' she muttered, after a while, half turning away, but he caught her by her shoulders before she could walk towards the bathroom and lock herself in.

She felt his hands on her shoulders, and instinctively she reached up to push them off.

Her brain had no time to warn her of the consequences of this simple action. She just knew that the feel of his skin on hers was unbearable, irresistible. A single touch and for some reason the issues in her brain became clouded, and she didn't want to be reduced to this state of fuzzy-headedness. She wanted to be able to think clearly, to breathe clearly.

She grabbed both his hands, panting as she did so, and in that split second the towel unravelled. She felt it slip off her, and the moment just seemed to go on for ever.

She struggled to pick it up, but he held her, propelling her towards the door so that her back was towards it, holding her arms slightly away from her body.

Jessica didn't dare look at him; she didn't dare look down at her state of nudity. She groaned in dismay and closed her eyes, sickly aware that his breathing had quickened.

A body disclosed bit by bit in a moment of passion was one thing. But to stand there, naked, to feel her breasts heavy and aching, to feel the throb of excitement spreading between her legs, to know that he was looking and taking it all in, was quite another matter.

Mortification swept over her in a flood, leaving her weak.

'You're quite beautiful,' he whispered huskily, and somehow the sound of his voice only made the situation worse.

She half opened her eyes and glanced down. Her nipples had hardened, and her breasts, their heaviness free from any encumbrance, were like two ripe fruits, offering themselves to him, waiting to be caressed and sucked.

She tried to think clearly, but her thoughts were foggy.

She wasn't so completely lost, however, that she didn't realise that this was a nightmare, a madness that had to stop. The problem was that she seemed incapable of doing anything about it. It was as though rational thought was only possible if she wasn't physically close to him.

She could rationalise her behaviour, excuse it, even, at a push, in the privacy of solitude. His presence seemed to paralyse her ability to reason, and his touch had the effect of a match being tossed onto a bundle of dry twigs.

She was no longer trying to escape. Her breathing had slowed, and when he released one hand she let it drop limply to her side.

She still didn't open her eyes, though, not until she felt his mouth circle her nipple, then she stared down at the bent head, confused at her inability to do anything but submerge herself in the moment.

'If you want me to stop, I'll stop,' he said, glancing up at her, his eyes dark, and she sighed.

'That's not good enough,' he said huskily, standing up and looking down at her. He tilted her head, and she gazed at him in a bleary-eyed way. 'The bed's behind me, the door's in front. Which direction do you want me to take?'

'I want to make love to you,' Jessica said. The bald simplicity of the statement was deafening. She heard it reverberate inside her head like a gong. She wrapped her arms around his head and pulled him towards her, kissing him fully on the mouth, a long, deep, hungry kiss that contained all the pent-up passion of a thousand years. She felt his tongue inside her mouth, and her decision not to allow her past to hold her back was like the sudden turning of a key and the opening of a door.

There was no resistance as he lifted her off her feet and carried her towards the bed.

No thoughts of Lucy, no thoughts of Fiona, no memories founded in fear. No thoughts at all.

She feverishly watched him undress, abandoning herself to the full impact of physical yearning, and as soon as he lay next to her she turned to him, moaning as his hands found her breasts, and he caressed them, massaged them, kissing her on the face and the neck as he did so.

Earlier, at the pool, the suddenness of her feelings had surprised her. There had been just that little corner of doubt in her mind, even when his mouth had roused her body to heat. Now there was no such doubt.

She lay back flat on the bed, with her arms on either side, and yielded to ferocious passion. His tongue played with her nipples, licking, teasing, arousing, while his fingers gently stroked her thighs. Her legs parted wider as she waited for him to move lower. He was in no hurry. He wanted to enjoy her. He guided her hand to his throbbing maleness, and she felt its stiffness with delight and a certain amount of fascinated trepidation.

His mouth absorbed her nipples deeper as she caressed him with longer, faster strokes. He was suckling hard on her now, and little spasms of electricity seemed to flood through her body. She couldn't keep still. What had started off at a leisurely pace picked up tempo, and she was groaning as his hands held her legs apart so that his mouth could explore between them.

She realised how frustrated he must have been earlier, when Lucy's interruption had summarily cut short their lovemaking. His desire must have been as great then as it clearly was now.

He thrust into her and she was ready for him, though not prepared first for that short burst of pain followed swiftly by a deep explosion of pleasure. His movements in her felt wonderful—wonderful and entirely new. Their bodies were moving as one.

My God, Jessica thought in wonder as they lay, assuaged, on the bed, I really was a virgin.

'Are you all right?' Those were the first words he asked, and she smiled at him drowsily.

'Very all right.' What happens now? The aftermath of lovemaking was not something she had experienced. In fact, lovemaking, she conceded, was not something she had ever experienced. She recoiled from the memory of Eric. 'What time is it?' she asked, and he smiled back at her.

'We have a little time before the chaperons return home.'

'I emphatically don't want Lucy to walk in unannounced...'

'She might get something of a shock,' he agreed, stroking her hair away from her face.

'That's putting it mildly.' Jessica relaxed, feeling his warmth against her like a comforting blanket. 'She looks the part of the rebel, but I suspect she's quite conventional under it all.'

'And, besides, teenagers can be hugely embarrassed at the thought of their parents making love.'

Teenagers, teenagers, teenagers. There was another thought at the back of her mind, struggling to find a way out.

She sat up abruptly and the colour drained from her face.

'Fiona,' she said, torn with conflicting emotions. 'What about Fiona? I was so carried away...'

'Relax.'

'Relax?' Jessica threw him a horrified, disbelieving look. 'I'm afraid I do have principles. One of them is not ever to get involved with anyone who's involved with someone else.' She could, she knew, have been slightly more truthful and stated that her principles actually included not getting involved with anyone at all, but that would have opened a whole big can of worms.

Eric Dean had been involved with someone else. Indeed, Eric Dean had been married to someone else, a fact that had only emerged as a throwaway remark while he'd been on his way out of the door and out of her life for ever.

She could still remember the shock she had felt at being so comprehensively duped, and the surge of sympathy she had felt for his poor wife, as much a victim as she had been.

'I'm not married to Fiona,' he said lazily, still not taking the conversation that seriously, still relaxed and soporific after their lovemaking.

'That's not the point. She's a part of your life, and...' Jessica sought around for the right way of expressing herself. 'And I won't be any part of...'

Anthony propped himself up on his elbows to look at

her. 'Fiona and I... It's not what you imagine,' he said, without any show of self-defence.

'That sounds very much like the married man who tells his mistress that his wife doesn't understand him.' She slipped off the bed and headed towards the wardrobe.

'Oh, for goodness' sake, come back here!'

Jessica ignored him and began getting dressed, and he shot out of the bed and pulled her back to it.

'Sit down and listen to me!' He propped her on the bed and held her there while she resisted him. Finally, realising that it was futile trying to match her strength against his, she remained quite still.

Events were taking over her life. There was no getting around it. Ever since this man had appeared on the scene, her thoughts and actions seemed to have gone haywire. On the surface, she looked the same, she spoke the same, but something inside her had changed. It was like one of those spooky horror movies where people's bodies were taken over by alien forces, so that nothing about them quite fitted together the way that it should.

He affected her. There was no other way to describe it. Why else would she react to him the way that she did, even though she knew that she shouldn't? Why else did her normally calm, unruffled life suddenly seem like a churning, unpredictable ocean most of the time? Why else had she started analysing her past, asking questions of herself? Why else had she suddenly begun to doubt things that she had previously taken for granted?

Why else had she slept with him? She couldn't quite believe that she had lost control to such an extent that she had forgotten all about Fiona.

Was she, she wondered, approaching some dreadful mid-life crisis a few years prematurely?

'I don't want to listen to you,' she said, with a catch in her voice.

'If I let you go, will you promise not to run away?'

Jessica nodded. What would be the point of running away? It was hardly as though she could leave, was it?

He got dressed, but kept his eyes on her, then he sat down on the chair by the bed and looked at her without smiling.

'What do you think is going on between Fiona and me?'

'It's obvious what's going on between the two of you. You may not be married, but you're as good as. And please don't misunderstand me. Apart from the fact that she's a bit on the young side, I'm sure you two are very well-matched...'

'You are?'

'Yes, and—'

'Why?'

'What?'

'Why do you think that we're very well-matched?'

'This is beside the point,' Jessica told him coldly. 'The point is, I let myself get... I wasn't thinking straight, but I'm just not the kind of woman who plays around with someone else's... I disapprove thoroughly of that. There's enough unhappiness in the world, as far as I'm concerned, without adding unnecessarily to it... It would look odd if I were to tell Lucy that we had to leave immediately, but I think that when we get back to London it would be preferable if...not that there's any reason why we should...even if...' She was, she realised, being completely incoherent, but he seemed to understand perfectly what she was saying.

And now, of all things, she felt tearful. Tearful! Tearful over a man whom she barely knew! It was ridiculous. She was thirty-three years old, for heaven's sake! She bit her lip and tucked her hair behind her ears; nervous gestures, she knew.

'You have completely misread a situation,' he told her calmly. 'Understandable, but true.'

'And what precisely *is* the situation?'

'I've known Fiona for years. She's always been like a kid sister to me, but recently...'

'She's blossomed and the "kid sister" description no longer fits?'

'Are you going to let me finish?'

They looked at one another in silence.

'Right,' he said. 'Don't interrupt. I like Fiona, but recently she's got it into her head that what is basically a next door neighbour relationship could develop into something else. She's infatuated with me. It's something she'll grow out of in due course.'

'Have you slept with her?'

'Would you be jealous if I had?'

Yes! 'No, I wouldn't, but I feel it's only fair that I know.'

'I have not slept with her. I have no idea how you could imagine that I would. No, I take that back. She's a very beautiful young woman, but a child as far as I'm concerned.'

She felt a rush of relief flood through her.

'We don't have an ongoing relationship. We will never have an ongoing relationship, and maybe I should have told her that bluntly three months ago, but I thought that lack of response would be sufficient. Frankly, she's a sweet kid and I didn't want to hurt her feelings. Now, does that answer your questions?'

'I guess so.' So, there was a host of other questions not too far in the distance, but surely she could overlook that just for the moment? Didn't she deserve a little bit of excitement and happiness in her life? Bringing up Lucy had been a joy, incomparable, but time was moving on. So what if Anthony Newman was unsuitable as a life partner? Was she even looking for a life partner?

She told herself that she wasn't.

'Anyway,' he was saying, and she looked at him with a lovely feeling of standing on the edge of an adventure, hazardous though the adventure might be. 'I don't think Fiona will be a problem from now on.'

'You mean that you're going to tell her about...tell her that you don't intend to become romantically involved with her?'

'I would, but I don't think it's going to be necessary.'

'Why not?' Jessica frowned, puzzled.

'Because I think she will have got the message by the fact that I've asked you up here for the weekend.' He half smiled.

'Is that why you asked me up?' Jessica said in a little voice. She frantically tried to remember every last detail of that conversation, and her memory was alarmingly accurate. Why else would he have made a point of asking her in front of Fiona? Why not have waited and phoned her a bit later? And he had changed the conversation when she had tried to explain that it was going to be purely platonic, an outing for the children, really.

He had planned the whole thing. Or rather he had thought on his feet, and no doubt had congratulated himself afterwards on his cleverness.

She felt the sour taste of disappointment in her mouth.

'So, in other words, you used me,' she said tightly, sickly.

'Of course I didn't use you. I saw an opportunity to

let Fiona know, as gently as possible, that I wasn't interested in her.'

'I see.'

'No, you don't!' he said angrily. 'You see what you want to see. I would never have suggested that you come up here for a weekend with Lucy if I basically didn't want you to. Dammit, Jessica, are you listening to me?'

The walls seemed to be closing in. Why had she let herself ever believe that this man had genuinely wanted her company? Why had she let herself be used again? She knew that she should be angry, but she wasn't. She just felt crushed.

'Well, I'm sure Lucy's enjoyed herself,' she said bravely.

'And you haven't?'

'It's been an experience.' She stood up to go downstairs. On the way, she would rescue her book from the dressing table, find a quiet place, she decided—there must be one in this sprawling mansion—and she would immerse herself in reading until her daughter returned.

'And you haven't?' He walked quickly behind her and held her arm, forcing her to look at him.

'You're hurting me.' In more ways than one, she thought bitterly.

'Answer me!' He waited, and she refused to oblige. 'I didn't plan on you and I ending up in bed together,' he grated, releasing her and standing back. 'I could understand that you might have felt exploited if I'd manoeuvred the situation with a view to seducing you, but I didn't.'

No, of course you didn't, she thought fiercely. Why on earth would you assume that you might possibly find me attractive? Fiona might be too young and too familiar for you, but your taste in women doubtless runs along those lines. I was here, though, and life's full of hiccups.

She thought of her restless, eager submission to him and cringed.

'I don't care what you say, Anthony Newman. You were an opportunist, and I don't like opportunists.'

'And I don't like being lumped into the same category as that man.'

'What man?'

'The man who put you in that ivory tower of yours and left you there so that you could observe life from the sidelines. Or maybe he didn't leave you there. Maybe you just decided to stay there of your own accord because it seemed the easy thing to do.'

'You don't know what you're talking about.'

They stared at each other for a while, and Jessica was the first to break it by snatching up her book and walking out of the bedroom. She hoped to God that he wasn't following her, but she didn't care.

She took the stairs two at a time and ferociously hunted down a small sitting room in the far corner of the house, where she curled up in a chair by the French window and stared out at the breathtaking view of perfectly cut grass and creatively manicured beds.

The book lay unopened on her lap. It was pointless even bothering to open it. She knew that she wouldn't be able to concentrate.

She could hardly think coherently. She kept expecting him to walk through the door, and her nerves were on edge, waiting, dreading.

But he didn't. Lucy was the first person to enter at a little after six. She flung herself into a chair, sprawled back with closed eyes and said with great feeling, 'I can't believe that I spent hours mooching around

Stratford. It was *crawling* with tourists, Mum. I haven't seen so many cameras outside a camera shop!' She opened one eye and promptly closed it. 'So, how was *your* afternoon?'

'Lucy!' Jessica injected disbelief into her voice. 'You're asking me about *my* day? I'm shocked.' She felt more normal now, with Lucy here giving her something else to think about. She realised that Lucy had always given her something else to think about. She had never really sat down and thought about herself and about the direction that her life was taking because she had always had other things on her mind. A baby, a young child, a job, childhood illnesses, her daughter's achievements and disappointments—a life of enjoyment, but also a life of coping.

Anthony Newman had forced her to see outside that world of coping into another world.

'I always ask you about your day, *Mother*.' She still had her eyes closed, but she was grinning. The country life obviously agreed with her more than she would ever have admitted.

'Ha!'

'Well, I always mean to, but before I can get to it you end up diverting me by nagging about homework or school or late nights or something else.'

'And so it's my fault! I might have guessed!' There was a grin in her voice.

'That's right. And—' Lucy looked at her with open speculation '—how did you and your host hit it off?' She adopted a phoney American accent. 'Did sparks ignite or did they fly? Tell all.'

'Lucy, really! Mr Newman is a very nice man.' She thought of his hands roaming over her body, his mouth on hers, demanding, and she resolutely kept her own eyes closed rather than subject herself to her daughter's inquisitive stare.

'A reasonable man, would you say?'

'I suppose. Why?' She opened her eyes and looked at her daughter suspiciously.

'Because perhaps you two could see your way to agreeing to allow Mark and I to spend three weeks away.'

'What?' Jessica sat bolt upright, fully alert now.

'Nothing sordid, Mum. You have a one-track mind.'

'I wasn't thinking anything of the sort! Three weeks away? Where?'

'Italy. Over the summer holidays.'

'Forget it, Luce!' Jessica thought of her daughter backpacking through Italy, hitching lifts from dubious lorry drivers, and her mind went blank with anxiety. There had been two school trips over the years—heavily supervised—and that was the extent of her daughter's travelling solo as far as she was concerned. Anything else would have to wait until she was much older.

'You haven't even heard me out!'

'I don't need to.'

'Why do you have to be so difficult?' Lucy's face had closed into that stubborn, rebellious look that Jessica knew so well.

'I'm only being protective.'

'But, Mum, it's not...'

'No, Luce! And, anyway, we simply can't afford that sort of trip for you. I'm sorry, but that's the end of the matter.' She sighed in frustration as her daughter flounced out of the room. Another headache, she thought. Will they ever end?

CHAPTER EIGHT

OVER the following fortnight, the subject of Italy was lost amidst a flurry of exams. Lucy barely seemed concerned about any of them. She sauntered out of the house every morning and returned to recount how she had done with an air of casual indifference. And for once Jessica allowed the show of indifference to wash over her. No prodding, no frustrated attempts to prise information out of her daughter. She was concerned, but not frantic, much—she could tell after a while—to Lucy's amazement.

'What's wrong with you, then?' her daughter demanded on the Thursday before the end of term. Lucy had cornered her at a little after nine in front of the television, and now stood at the door with her arms folded and an expression of weary persistence on her face.

'Just relaxing,' Jessica told her with some surprise. 'I thought you were going out with your friends to celebrate the end of exams.'

'I *am* going out with my friends,' Lucy told her. 'A bit later.'

'Oh, right. Should I stay up for you?' The very late nights had recently been abandoned. Lucy told her that she was bored with the same faces in the same places, but Jessica suspected that she was too busy studying, though she knew better than to contradict her daughter's explanation.

138

'No reason to. You know you always hit the roof whatever time I get back.'

'Right ho, then, darling; I'll hit the sack now, in that case.' She switched off the television and began stacking the newspapers on her lap into a bundle. She had no idea why she bothered buying two newspapers. Lately she never managed to get through one, far less both of them. Too much on her mind and too much energy spent trying to avoid thinking about things.

'You've been acting a bit odd,' Lucy said in an accusatory voice.

'Odd, darling? What on earth do you mean?'

'Well, for starters, you haven't lectured me about passing these exams…' Lucy glared at her mother.

'I just hope that you did your best, Luce.' She felt a twinge of guilt that she had spent the last couple of weeks letting her daughter get on with things instead of helping her with her revision.

'Well, whatever,' Lucy shrugged and continued to stare implacably at her mother. 'You've been different ever since that weekend in Dullsville.'

Lucy had adopted that nickname for their weekend in the country with Mark and Anthony—never mind that she appeared to have thoroughly enjoyed the place.

'Have I?' Jessica looked vaguely around her, gathering up final bits of discarded newspaper.

The last thing she wanted to discuss was that weekend at Elmsden House. She had thought of nothing else for the past two weeks. She went to bed at night thinking of Anthony Newman and she woke up the following morning thinking of him. It was as though his image had taken root in her mind and started growing.

At work she was distracted. The smallest of jobs seemed to require inordinate amounts of concentration, and by the time five-thirty rolled around she couldn't wait to leave. But then, once home, she found herself wishing that she was back at work, where at least the routine went a little way towards taking her mind off things.

'Yes, you have. And could you *please* try and pay me some attention when I'm talking to you?' Mother and daughter looked at one another, and Lucy was the first to look away with an expression of sheepishness on her face at the outburst.

'I'll do my very best,' Jessica said lightly. 'Is it all right if I take these newspapers to the kitchen? This sitting room looks like a tip, and I have to be out of the house by seven tomorrow morning.'

'And who's going to do my breakfast?' Lucy demanded, distracted by the prospect of having to fend for herself.

'Well, with me not in the house, I guess that just leaves one of us!' Jessica headed towards the kitchen with the bundle of newspapers in her arms, stacked them into a cardboard box—currently brimming over with newspapers which should have been disposed of at least a week ago—and then began wiping the counters. Quickly, efficiently.

'Ha, ha.'

'Well, Luce, I don't suppose you've got to arrive too early for school, if your exams are all over. You'll have more than enough time to fix yourself something.'

'Why do you have to leave so early for work?'

'I'm behind.' She was too. For the first time ever. She would have to get her act together.

'Aren't there rules about working those unsocial hours?' Lucy sat down on a kitchen stool and sniffed loudly. 'Some law handed down from Brussels?'

'No.'

'Anyway, you've changed, and I know why.'

Jessica stopped in mid-wipe and stared at her daughter worriedly. She had tried to make sure that she gave nothing away. She felt enough of a fool without drawing attention to her stupidity. The remainder of that nightmarish weekend had passed amid pleasantries. She had been a perfectly polite guest; she had carefully hidden the fact that she had been dying to leave, to get away from Anthony Newman's stifling, disturbing presence.

It hadn't been easy. She had felt his eyes on her, brooding, watching, and she had resolutely made sure to avoid any possible opportunity for him to talk to her on a one-to-one basis.

And since then his name had not been mentioned.

'Why?' she asked in a casual voice. She sat down, though. Her legs felt shaky.

'It's that Italy trip, isn't it?' Lucy scowled. 'It's been preying on your mind!'

'We've been through this, Lucy.' Jessica breathed a little inward sigh of relief. Not, she thought, that she had much to be relieved about. She had considered Italy a closed affair. Now here it was, rearing its head again.

'You didn't even hear what I had to say!'

'I don't need to.'

'You never *listen*.'

'Look, darling…' Jessica spoke clearly, firmly and kindly. 'I have no idea which one of you two thought of this little adventure, but it doesn't matter. I don't care for the thought of you going to Italy with Mark Newman, however nice I find him…'

'Why?'

'Because I just don't.' It was the most feeble piece of

reasoning she had ever heard in her life, but it was also the safest way of closing the discussion.

'Is it the money thing?'

'No, although that's a small technical hitch, wouldn't you say?'

'If you lent me the money, I'd pay you back…'

'No. End of discussion.'

Lucy muttered something inaudible under her breath, and Jessica clicked her tongue impatiently. She wasn't in the mood for this repetitive, pointless discussion about a trip that wasn't going to materialise. But, still, she felt badly about it in a way. To be a teenager again, fighting against an implacable parent… If only she could make her daughter understand how preferable that was to living with indifference.

The matter was dropped, but the atmosphere was uneasy. To clear the air would involve broaching the subject again, and Jessica really didn't know if this was the best way forward. It would either lead to Lucy appreciating why she couldn't go, or else it would just simply further her stubborn feeling of being overruled. She couldn't take the chance.

But it gnawed away at her until she decided, on the spur of the moment one week later, that she would do something about it—to make up for Lucy's disappointment. She returned from work, grinning for the first time in weeks, with a handful of brochures. Spain, Portugal and Greece. Mother and daughter, a week's rest in the sunshine somewhere, close to a beach, close to a swimming pool. An olive branch.

The house was empty.

Jessica didn't even think about Lucy's absence. At least not for a couple of hours. She assumed that her daughter was with a friend. She prepared dinner, pottered, grew more anxious as she looked at the hands on the clock ticking by.

By eight she was telling herself to keep calm, but within half an hour she had telephoned Lucy's friends and it was only when she met with blank responses that she began to feel ill.

Should she telephone the police? She sat in the kitchen with the brochures dumped on the table in a disorderly pile in front of her, and supported her head in her hands.

Had Lucy even returned home after school? Her mind raced ahead to possible scenarios. Her daughter returned home—tall, leggy, her hair swinging around her face. From a distance, a self-confident young woman, not the often gauche girl she was. A temptation for some depraved man who happened to be travelling back on the same route. She squeezed her eyes tightly shut and bit her clenched knuckles.

But if she had returned home her uniform would be in the bedroom.

Jessica hurried to check. Lucy's bedroom was as she might have expected it to be—bed roughly made, curtains half-drawn. School uniform in a bundle by the dressing table.

She walked in. Something didn't quite add up.

The wardrobe doors were open and clothes were missing. Jessica could see that at a glance. She feverishly checked and rechecked. By the time her mind had arrived at its conclusion, the contents of the note on the dressing table were virtually redundant.

Lucy had gone to Italy for three weeks.

I know you're going to be furious, but it was a chance in a lifetime, and I haven't been anywhere as exciting in my life before.

As though, Jessica thought with mounting anger, she had kept her daughter trapped within four walls and fed her on bread and water for the past sixteen years.

She didn't wait to think. She picked up the telephone, dialled Anthony Newman's number, and with a *déjà vu* feeling waited for it to be answered.

'I need to see you,' she said, as soon as his voice came down the line. The timbre of it didn't reduce her to morbid, cringing introspection. Her urgency had put paid to that, at least for the moment.

'Have you ever thought of adopting a more polite approach in these sorts of circumstances?'

'Right now. Lucy's gone.'

'Gone? Gone where?' He spoke sharply.

'To Italy. I've only just discovered a note she left lying on her dressing table.'

'I'll kill him if he's persuaded her to go with him,' Anthony said grimly. 'I'm afraid I had no idea. I'll get to you immediately.' He hung up, and Jessica was left holding the telephone, which she slowly replaced after a while.

She reread the note. 'I'll call,' it said, 'as soon as I arrive.' Knowing her daughter, that probably meant that she would call just as soon as she thought that her mother's wrath had abated.

I could strangle her, she thought. Now that her fears of abduction were gone, anxiety was giving way to anger. Wasn't this just typical of her headstrong daughter? She thought of Mark coercing Lucy into the trip, and realised that the truth was probably a little different. He had, she acknowledged to herself, probably tried to dissuade her. But Lucy could be as stubborn as a mule, and she had obviously made up her mind to go and off she'd gone.

Where on earth had she got the money? No doubt from her building society account, which Jessica had been adding to over the years, building up a nest-egg for Lucy's college days. She didn't want even to think about that.

By the time the doorbell rang, her head was beginning to hurt.

She yanked open the door, looked at the tall, still alarmingly handsome face looking back at her, and felt even more enraged.

'Can you believe it?' were her opening words. 'When I get my hands on that daughter of mine, I'm going to throttle her! I've spent the past four hours worried sick!'

'May I come in?'

His voice was utterly calm. It was like having cool water poured over her.

Jessica stepped back, leaving him to shut the door behind him, and headed for the sitting room.

'Has she phoned?' he asked, once they were both sitting down.

'No.' Jessica stared glumly at him, half wishing that she hadn't bothered to call him, resenting the fact that even with her mind preoccupied with Lucy she still couldn't help drinking him in. This awful, powerful, helpless attraction was the closest she had ever come to an addiction, and she wished that she could turn it off.

'Had she discussed the idea with you?'

'No. Yes.' She blushed a little. 'Sort of.'

'Sort of…?'

'Well, it's all very well for you to send your son to Italy, but firstly he's a boy, and secondly I just couldn't see that I could afford the luxury!'

Anthony coolly ignored the accusation behind the outburst. 'So she did mention the subject to you?'

'And I told her no. Categorically.' In fact, she thought, there really hadn't been any discussion at all. She had simply put her foot down the way she'd used to when Lucy had been very young and had asked for something preposterous. She was slowly coming round to the idea that dictatorship was a thing of the past, and she half closed her eyes with a sudden wave of guilt. She should at least have had a rational conversation about the whole thing.

'I brought details of where Mark's staying.' He handed her a slip of paper, which she looked at. It meant nothing at all to her. She had never been to Italy, did not speak Italian, and had no idea where this so-called place was. North? West? South? Somewhere in the middle?

'Is this the first stop on a tour? When Lucy brought up the subject, I just assumed that…' Her voice faltered.

'That she was going to be hitch-hiking her way around the country with my son, vulnerable to the passing whim of some crazed lorry driver…?'

He had so accurately hit the nail on the head that she felt a rush of defensive, righteous anger flood through her.

'Mothers tend to be just a *little* protective of their girls, *Mr Newman*!'

'I realise that.' He sighed, raked his fingers through his hair, and looked at her with such brooding directness that she could feel her body begin to burn.

'I very much doubt it. I'll bet you just nodded when Mark suggested the idea, threw some money at him, and then forgot about the whole thing.'

'He's no longer a child.'

'And Lucy is!' Maybe not, though. Maybe she was leaving childhood behind, and the way to deal with that wasn't to try and keep her where she was, but simply to build their relationship up in a slightly different way.

'Well, there's no point arguing the toss. There's a phone number listed. Why don't you just give her a call and put your mind at rest?'

'My mind isn't going to be at rest just by speaking to her down the end of a line! How do I know what kind of place this is?' She stared at the slip of paper, as though hopeful that the words would somehow rearrange themselves into something comprehensible. 'What kind of place is this anyway?'

Anthony shrugged. 'A campus of sorts, I gather…'

'A campus? Of sorts? Don't you mean a commune…?'

'I don't think it's quite what you have in mind.'

'How do you know what I have in mind?'

'Because your face is as transparent as glass.' He looked at her and she felt that tingle of awareness zip through her again, like an electric shock. Brief but potent.

She had, she considered, never been told that she was transparent. Just the opposite. Funny thing was that with Anthony Newman it was as though he could read her mind, as though he had somehow discovered an inside route through the workings in her head. In a way, as though they had known one another for centuries.

'I don't think it's a collection of hippies—picking grapes, tilling the land and participating in orgies at night…' A sudden flash of humour crossed his face, and she unwillingly felt it suffuse her like incense.

'Well, what sort of place is it, then?'

'I gather it's some sort of art place…'

'What's a ''some sort of art place''?'

He shrugged again, as though uncomfortable with her

detailed questioning. 'Well, I didn't exactly read the damned brochure back to front, Jessica. Like I said to you, Mark's a big boy now, quite capable of taking care of himself.'

'You mean that you switched off the minute you heard that it had to do with art.'

He scowled at her but didn't say anything.

They were arguing. Again. Yet there was a strange undercurrent of intimacy behind the argument, and she wondered whether she was the only one feeling it.

More than likely, she thought. Far more probable was that he considered her a mumsy bore, bristling and defending her daughter like an anxious mother hen. Again. The desperate, clinging parent who refused to acknowledge that there came a time for letting go.

'Mark mentioned in passing that there's teaching on the premises. I just let him get on with it. I had no idea that Lucy was involved.'

'I shall have to go and see what all this is about,' Jessica told him eventually. She smoothed the piece of paper and tried to work out how much the trip would cost. Well, it didn't matter.

'I thought you might say that.'

'What a mind-reader,' she mumbled under her breath.

'So I got my secretary to get us on the next flight over, which is tomorrow morning.'

Jessica's head shot up and she stared at him, dumbfounded.

'You did what…?'

'I have a breakfast meeting, but I'll meet you at the airport at ten-thirty.'

'You'll do nothing of the sort!' she spluttered.

'We should be there some time after lunch. We can sort out accommodation once we arrive.'

'You're not listening to me! I don't want to go with you. *You weren't invited.*'

'I fail to see how you can keep me off the plane,' Anthony told her reasonably, but his eyes were cold, as though he had sized up her reaction and knew precisely what lay behind it. 'I feel slightly responsible for Mark involving your daughter in all this.'

'Well, don't,' Jessica said abruptly, but he was already standing up. Business finished. How, in such a short time, had she and her daughter somehow managed to become this man's responsibility? She had always prided herself on her independence, which now seemed to be compromised. She didn't want Anthony Newman treating them as though they were charity cases which had to be sorted out.

'I only wanted you to tell me where they were staying!' she protested heatedly as he walked towards the front door. 'I didn't want you becoming *involved.* I'm more than capable of handling things from here on!'

'You have a problem accepting help.'

'I never had any of these problems until you came along!' she informed him, swerving around him so that she barred his exit through the front door. She folded her arms and stared at him without flinching.

He looked back at her with an odd expression.

'Funny. I could say exactly the same thing. My life was relatively problem-free until you appeared.'

It wasn't what she had expected to hear, and she blinked back a mixture of hurt and anger.

'I'll see you tomorrow at the airport,' he said, pushing her to one side and opening the front door.

Maybe, she thought viciously, or maybe not. Maybe I'll just make a phone call and let Lucy get on with whatever it is she's doing there. But she knew that she would do no such thing. Years of protectiveness were very hard to do away with.

Lucy could be at a kibbutz, or an establishment of high learning with segregated floors—she had to go; she had to see for herself. She knew that she couldn't just let go and hope for the best. Other parents might joyfully be able to send their teenage girls away for three weeks abroad with only the occasional phone call to let them know that everything was all right, but not her. Lucy was her life.

The thought, which she took to bed, was a faintly depressing one. She would have to wean herself away from this protectiveness. Sooner or later she would be on her own.

So she was there at the airport the following morning, in sandals and a dress, and with a small case stuffed with various bits of clothing, a book and some make-up. She had no idea how long she would be in Italy, but she didn't envisage that it would be longer than a couple of days. Nor did she envisage what she would say to her daughter when they did meet. That was a headache which she would have to face when the time came.

Anthony didn't arrive until the plane was ready to board, which further increased her already disgruntled frame of mind.

'Sorry,' he said briefly, going through all the airport technicalities with the knowhow of someone who's quite familiar with the procedure and heartily bored by it all. 'Last-minute things to sort out.'

'You needn't have bothered,' Jessica told him, breathlessly following him as he wound his way through the terminal and towards the gate where the plane was boarding.

It felt peculiar not to be in charge. Even more peculiar was the fact that she found it refreshing, even though the circumstances were awful and his presence on the scene, she told herself, was little more than interference.

'I called Mark last night,' he said as they were led to their seats.

Jessica looked around her, forgetting for a moment that she truly resented him being here with her. 'We're travelling first class,' she whispered to him, sitting down and stretching out her legs in front of her. It was luxurious. Lots of space, not many people sharing the compartment, and an air of deference as the air hostess offered them a glass of champagne.

'Oh, so we are.'

She surreptitiously checked out the various buttons on the armrests, tempted to push them all just to see what they would do.

'You can press them all just as soon as the plane's in the air,' he told her, *sotto voce*, and she turned to see him looking at her with an expression of amusement.

'You were saying?' Jessica reminded him haughtily. 'You telephoned your son…?'

'And he said that Lucy showed up unexpectedly. Apparently she decided to go on the spur of the moment.'

'The little minx,' Jessica muttered. 'Stubborn as a mule.'

'She must get it from somewhere,' Anthony commented neutrally, but she let that remark go.

'She's in for a shock when she sees me.' Jessica tried to picture the look on her daughter's face and couldn't.

'And what do you intend to do once the shock's worn off?' Anthony asked bluntly. 'Haul her onto the next flight out, kicking and screaming?'

If I think that's the right thing to do,' Jessica told him acidly. 'I certainly have no intention of leaving her in some free-loving community to her own devices.'

'You have no idea what the place is going to be like. You're merely jumping to erroneous conclusions. Do you ever give anyone or anything the benefit of the doubt? Or do you think that would be setting a dangerous precedent?'

Jessica looked away and gritted her teeth together. They were in the air. Land had been left behind, and the clouds underneath resembled a bed of pillows. It had been such a long time since she had been on a plane, way back in the distant days of her childhood when her parents had taken her to Portugal where they had waged a silent war for a week. Now she wished that she hadn't always opted for the safety of holidays in Britain. She wished that she had just blown the money now and again and taken Lucy to some place across the seas, just to feel this excitement at the prospect of leaving one country behind and arriving at another.

'I refuse to argue with you,' she said, closing her eyes and enjoying the sensation of being in the air. She could feel him staring at her. Unnerving.

They passed the flight in relative silence. She read her book. He pulled a stack of papers out of his briefcase and became lost in whatever they were about. Jessica had no idea. She glanced over at them a couple of times. They all looked massively complicated.

It was only when they had landed and were being taxied to the address on the slip of paper left for his father by Mark that Jessica realised how calm she was. Still worried, still angry, but not nearly as frantic as she would have been had she been making the trip on her own.

She gazed out of the car window, while in the background Anthony conversed in very passable Italian to the taxi driver, and wondered whether single-handedly raising Lucy had turned her into that worst of all possible things—the over-protective mother. Would she have been different if she had had someone around to share things with?

'How much further?' she asked, looking at Anthony, somehow resenting the fact that she was grateful that he was sitting next to her.

'Few minutes,' the taxi driver said, catching her eye in the rear-view mirror, seemingly proud of his knowledge of the English language.

Jessica scowled, and Anthony, who was looking at her, said in a cool voice, 'You might as well relax. There's no point in getting over-excited about something that's already happened. Lucy's here, and you've got no option but to accept the fact.'

Oh, very easy for you to say! she thought, ignoring his unwanted advice. Mark's well able to take care of himself and, in all events, you probably don't care one way or another anyway. Lord knows, you washed your hands of him long ago.

The thought was so uncharitable that she turned away and resumed her inspection of the scenery flashing past them. They appeared to be heading into nothing. They had been driving for what seemed like days, going at an abnormally sedate pace, and now there was open countryside all around them, bathed in sunlight.

A 'few minutes' turned out to be anything but a few minutes. Anthony appeared utterly unconcerned, and the taxi driver was rattling on about the surroundings in rapid Italian. It was hopeless even trying to interpret what he was saying. Her only knowledge of the Italian language were the words 'Cornetto' and *'mamma mia'*.

Anthony asked him a question, and, after listening to the answer, he said to her that the nearest hotel was at least forty-five minutes' drive away.

'And there's no guarantee that there'll be rooms available. Apparently there are two hotels, for want of a better word, and there's a local festival of sorts taking place this week so there's a good chance that everywhere will be fully booked.'

'You mean we'll have to head back this evening?' Jessica asked him in some dismay. She felt hot and sticky and tired.

Anthony shrugged. 'Unless this place has spare rooms.'

She contemplated the prospect of no accommodation in silence.

'I guess I could always squeeze into Lucy's room,' she said finally. 'And you can sleep with Mark.'

'I don't think that would be suitable,' Anthony informed her, resting his hand over his knee and staring at her.

'Why not?'

'In case you haven't noticed, Mark and I don't see eye to eye on quite a number of things.'

Jessica fully turned so that she was facing him.

'And don't give me that look,' he grated.

'What look?'

'The look that tells me that you're about to climb onto your bandwagon of lecturing me on the importance of bonding with one's offspring.'

There wasn't time to reply to that. They were drawing up, quite suddenly, it seemed, to a clearing amidst the rolling countryside, turning left, and then there it was.

Nothing at all as Jessica had pictured. A large block, with offshoots on both sides, and an air of learning. Or at least an air of activity. Groups of young people strolled around the grounds, and she scoured them for Lucy.

'I can feel your blood pressure rising,' Anthony said dryly from next to her.

'My blood pressure is fine,' Jessica returned, squinting and trying to spot Lucy's familiar shape. 'I don't guarantee what it's going to be like once I'm through with Luce, but right now I've very relaxed.'

'I'd hate to see you if you were tense.'

'Ha, ha,' she said distractedly.

The taxi driver pulled up outside the building amidst yet more rapid Italian, removed their bags from the boot of the car and, almost before she could turn around, was rattling off away from the place.

'I feel about a hundred,' Jessica said to Anthony, not looking at him. The average age group of the people she could see milling around—most of them with books or portfolios under their arms—looked to be about nineteen. Several were eying them with curiosity, as though they were weird dinosaurs that had somehow been transported through time.

'You don't look it,' Anthony told her, picking up both their bags and striding into the building, unconcerned. She followed him inside, still looking for a glimpse of Lucy, and allowed him to handle the question-and-answer torrent which started off in broken English on the part of the woman behind the reception desk, then quickly changed to Italian as soon as she realised that Anthony was fluent in the language.

'We can leave our bags here,' he said eventually, turning to Jessica. 'And we can try the studio for them, or else the refectory.'

'The refectory,' Jessica said promptly, thinking of Lucy's gargantuan appetite.

'And, by the way, they can squeeze us in for a couple of nights if we want.'

'Squeeze us in?'

'There aren't many rooms, but they're going to do a bit of reshuffling.'

Jessica breathed a sigh of relief. One problem solved. Now just one left to go.

CHAPTER NINE

JESSICA had no idea how this place would be classified. Too small for a proper university, but too big for a school. Definitely not a commune, though, and that in itself was reassuring. The people, she thought with relief, looked *normal*. No one appeared to be salivating at the mouth, and there were no dubious chants emerging from behind suspiciously closed doors.

It occurred to her that if she had listened to what her daughter had been saying, if she had shown the slightest bit of interest instead of simply refusing point-blank to broach the subject, then she might have been more capable of making a rational, informed decision on the matter.

She suddenly saw herself through her daughter's eyes, and the sight was not a particularly happy one.

'Did you know that it would be like this?' she asked tentatively, taking in the surroundings.

Anthony shrugged, as though he had given the matter little thought and was, anyway, bored by such speculation.

'I knew that it wasn't a hell-hole of rampant sex.'

'But beyond that you weren't overly concerned.' She glanced sideways at him and felt the energy radiating out of him, that strange, restless, captivating power that attracted and infuriated at the same time.

She felt a sudden, impatient urge to shake him, make him see that he was wasting an opportunity with his son, to tell him that if he wasn't careful the opportunity might well just slip through his fingers, never to be recaptured. Mark was still at an age when parental blessing would matter, whether he said so or not. In a few years' time he would probably cease to care, and then the distance between them would be virtually unbreachable.

Does it matter, though? she thought. Does it really matter whether he gets along with his son or not? And, uneasily, she thought that it did. Inexplicably.

'The refectory's just along here, if I understood the moustached lady correctly,' he said, neatly sidestepping her question.

They entered a large, packed room. At one end was a bar of sorts, around which several dozen students hovered like a collection of bees buzzing around a pot of honey. Alongside it was a door, through which she could see tables and chairs laid out in charmless, utilitarian rows, and she guessed that hot food was probably served there.

The rest of the room was sprinkled with chairs here and there and the odd table. In the centre, a couple of steps led down to an area where yet more students were sitting on the ground conversing, with those peculiarly intent expressions of young adults. No doubt setting the world to rights.

Jessica's eyes flicked around the room and finally found what they were looking for. She nudged Anthony's elbow and pointed to a small group. Lucy and Mark both had their backs to them, and Lucy, as she had expected, appeared to be eating.

She felt a rush of affection, and said, shakily, 'Shall we make our presence known?'

'I suppose we might just as well, now that we're here.'

'You sound reluctant,' she said sharply, turning to look up at him, and he raised his eyebrows.

'You're projecting your own feelings onto me,' he commented mildly, at which she frowned.

'You needn't come with me,' she told him stiffly, blushing. 'You're happy enough that Mark's here, and Lucy is hardly any concern of yours.'

He clicked his tongue in annoyance, though he didn't look annoyed. More exasperated. The way she knew she sometimes looked when Lucy dug her heels in over something silly. It was a look guaranteed to make her feel like a child, and she pulled herself up with a dignified expression.

'Come along,' he said, touching her elbow lightly, then quickly allowing his hand to fall to his side. 'Let's go and get this over with.'

It was a question of wending their way, attracting the occasional glance of curiosity, but on the whole passing unnoticed.

In fact, the three young people in the group with Mark and Lucy didn't acknowledge their presence at all until Jessica said, brightly, 'Lucy!'

Lucy turned around, and Jessica continued to force a smile on her face as she watched the colour steadily creep into her daughter's cheeks.

'Mum!' she said in dismay, then she lowered her voice. 'What are you doing here?'

'Just passing by, so I thought I'd drop in,' Jessica quipped, which didn't elicit the slightest return of humour. Mark, she noticed out of the corner of her eye, had greeted his father with a noticeable lack of enthusiasm, and appeared equally embarrassed by the presence of his parent.

'*Please* don't make a scene,' Lucy hissed, looking furtively around her as though she might be recognised.

Since they were in a foreign country, that seemed highly unlikely to Jessica.

'I wasn't about to!' Jessica told her.

'And *please* could you keep your voice down?' Lucy grabbed Jessica by the arm and whispered frantically, 'I think we ought to clear out of here. It's far too crowded for conversation.'

'I'm not going to embarrass you, Luce!' Jessica said, affronted. 'I mean, I promise I won't raise my voice or gesticulate too much or do a striptease on one of those plastic tables.' Out of the corner of her eye she could see Anthony stifle a grin, and she felt a sudden empathy with him, a sudden feeling of irrational closeness that defied description.

'Mum! Everyone's *staring*.'

'Who?'

'They're going to think that...'

'Who's going to think what?' Jessica asked, perplexed.

'Perhaps we'd all better just move along outside,' Anthony said in an exaggeratedly conspiratorial voice which made Lucy frown.

'I really would prefer some privacy with my mother, Mr Newman,' she said loftily, which rendered him temporarily speechless.

'Yes.' Jessica looked at him briefly and their eyes met in perfect, tacit understanding, which he found not in the least to his liking. 'You stay with Mark. Perhaps...' she looked enquiringly at Mark '..you could show your father where you're working... He did mention to me on the plane that it was about time he took more of an interest in your art...'

'He did? Ha.'

Anthony was no longer looking at her. His hands were

firmly stuck in his pockets, and he was glaring at the tips of his shoes. She hardly needed to see his face to know that that was his expression.

It was, she had to admit, a low trick, but Mark needed him whether he could see that or not, and, besides, the opportunity had been just too impossible to resist.

She walked off, with Lucy's arm firmly linked through hers, as though her daughter was scared that at any minute her mother would do something horrendously, embarrassingly unpredictable. And in exceedingly bad taste.

'I wouldn't have minded something to drink,' Jessica said as they walked away from the refectory.

'I have a kettle in my room. Mum, *what* on *earth* are you *doing* here?'

'You didn't expect me just to shrug my shoulders when I read that note of yours, did you?'

'I told you that I would call!'

'I was worried sick, Lucy. Have you any idea how irresponsible it was of you just to vanish, without a word?'

'Please don't launch into one of your speeches, Mum,' Lucy said miserably. 'I would have told you, but you would probably have locked me in the bedroom!'

'Don't be ridiculous!'

They were walking quickly, purposefully, though where exactly they were heading Jessica was unclear about.

Once outside, however, in the warm, breezy air, she stopped and said, 'Let's go sit under that tree and talk, Lucy.'

'Only if you promise not to start shouting.'

'I never shout!'

'All right, then, *shout*'s the wrong word. *Use that voice* is probably what I mean.'

'What voice?'

'The one that was fine to use when I was five years old and needed reprimanding.' But not now, her expression implied, and Jessica tacitly took the point without objecting.

'I just wish you'd told me what you were planning to do,' she said, on a sigh, and sat down under the tree, tucking her legs underneath her.

'I would have,' Lucy said, sitting down as well and holding her face up to the sun like a flower. 'I tried. You don't understand. I really *wanted* to come here. Not just because it sounded like fun, but because I needed to…be free.'

'Are you trying to say that I smother you?' Jessica tried to sound light-hearted about that, but something inside her turned over. Was this what letting go felt like? Shouldn't it have been a gradual sort of process?

Lucy blushed, but didn't deny it.

'I only try…' Jessica heard her voice sound exactly how she'd hoped it never would. Self-pitying, bewildered.

'I know,' Lucy said quickly.

'But, you're right. Absolutely right. You're not a baby any longer.' She stroked her daughter's hair and thought how good it felt to feel close without the inevitable arguments rising to the fore. 'Of course, you'll *always* be my baby, but you'll be entitled to vote soon, drive a car…'

'Does that mean that you'll pay for some driving lessons for me?' Lucy asked eagerly, jumping on the bandwagon with breathtaking speed.

'It's a distinct possibility.' She restrained herself from

adding that only if the car she eventually bought had an engine the size of a sewing machine.

'And does that mean that I can stay here? That you won't haul me back home?'

'Well…' Jessica glanced around her. 'Looks a safe enough place to me, I guess. And independence has to start somewhere.' She stood up and pulled Lucy to her feet. 'Now, shall we head back in?'

'Rescue Mark from his father?' She shot her mother one of those childishly adult looks from under her lashes. 'What's he doing here anyway?'

'He came to make sure that Mark—'

'And pigs fly!' She snickered meaningfully. 'Are you sure he didn't jump at the excuse to be next to you?'

'Don't be ludicrous!'

Jessica could feel herself growing hot under the collar. Her instinct was to launch into full-denial mode, in fact to explain why her daughter couldn't be further from the truth, but too many protestations, she knew, would only have the opposite effect. She still didn't dare meet Lucy's eyes, though. Too much risk of her seeing the thousand guilty, confused thoughts in her mind.

'I think he felt responsible for you because he had no idea that you were going to come over here without permission. In fact, he had no idea that you were involved in the scenario at all.' Her voice bordered on the stilted.

'Oh, *really*? Sure you're not leaving out anything?'

'Lucy!'

Lucy laughed and let the subject drop, and they strolled back towards the refectory, where there was no sign of either father or son. So they moved on.

Lucy showed her around the place, which was smaller though more comprehensive than Jessica had first thought, ending up at her bedroom—a small affair but with, at any rate, the virtue of being private—and then on to the art block, which Lucy had been saving for last.

It was large and fairly meandering, and, with the guileless pride of the young, Lucy led Jessica, first stop, to the room where she took art classes.

'I have no talent whatsoever,' she announced honestly, gazing at the series of unidentifiable line drawings on one of the desks. 'But it's fun having a go.'

Jessica picked up the thick paper and held it at different angles, bemused as to what it was supposed to represent.

'Abstract,' her daughter said helpfully. 'We're encouraged to let our feelings speak on paper.'

'Right.' Would it be offensive to ask what feelings these various lines represented? Jessica wondered.

'But I seem to like drawing lines and angles. Hangover from being so good at maths,' Lucy continued, reading her thoughts.

Jessica smiled affectionately at the frowning, attractive, dark-haired teenager at her side. For the first time in ages she felt comfortable with her daughter, and it was a good feeling.

When she next looked up, it was to see Mark and Anthony strolling towards them, and her heart did its usual thing—stopped beating for a couple of seconds—then restarted, but in overdrive. Or at least that was the way it seemed to feel.

She could feel Lucy looking at her, and she casually smiled at the two approaching figures.

'Where were you?' Lucy asked Mark, who accepted the lack of pleasantries with a good-humoured grin. 'We went back to the refectory, but you were gone. I still haven't had my pudding.'

'You ate three rolls an hour ago, Lucy. Aren't you in

danger of exploding?' They grinned at one another, for all the world like two siblings who had no use for politeness.

'Fancy something to eat, you two?' She looked at Jessica and Anthony with a Mona Lisa type of smile. 'Or does cafeteria food not meet with your high standards?' This she addressed with raised eyebrows to Anthony, who tried to keep a straight face.

'I think we'll try something local in the nearest town,' Anthony said, ignoring the question.

'Will we?' Jessica looked at him and cleared her throat.

'We will. Mark tells me that you two have classes in an hour's time. You might as well take yourselves off and—' he glanced with amusement at Lucy '—eat to your heart's content until then.'

They sauntered off, and Jessica turned to Anthony and informed him that she wasn't very hungry.

'I lose my appetite when I'm feeling stressed,' she said lamely. He had somehow worked his way into her life. Why bother denying it? These past few weeks had been hellishly difficult, and that was simply because she'd missed him. Now that circumstance had once more tossed them into the same boiling pot, it was useless to think that she could fight the attraction she had for him. The best she could hope to do was to minimise it. And that involved avoiding a quiet lunch with him at some local tavern.

'Why should you still be feeling stressed?' he asked her bluntly, and, without giving her much time to find an answer, he took her by the elbow and led her towards the front of the building. 'You've tracked your daughter down and from the looks of it things haven't gone too badly between you. So explain where these stress levels are coming from. I'm dying to know.'

'Where are you taking me? I don't like being frog-marched.'

'In addition to which,' he continued, exasperatingly ignoring her input, 'you're in a foreign country, and a particularly beautiful one at that. The weather is splendid and you must be starving.'

'We don't have a car. We can't go anywhere.' And you're under no obligation to entertain me, she wanted to add. If you liked my company that much, how was it that you never tried to contact me? Not even a phone call? That thought stuck in her throat like a bitter stone, and it didn't matter that she had expressly told him that she was not interested in what he had to offer. Did I even cross your busy mind once? she wanted to ask.

'Taxis, exist, I believe. Contactable by telephone. Of which there most definitely are a few on this campus, including one at the reception area.'

'In other words, you intend to get your own way.'

'In other words.' Their eyes met briefly and she felt faint. Where was her sharp tongue and independent spirit when she needed them? Just round the corner, she supposed, having a tea break.

'Any objections?' he persisted, and when she didn't say anything he nodded with satisfaction. 'Good.'

She stifled all the petulant questions. What would have been the point of asking them? Apart from to reveal how vulnerable she was to him, how much, quite simply, he mattered.

The moustached, middle-aged woman on the reception desk was obliging, Jessica noticed sourly, to the point of flirtatiousness. And Anthony, making the very most of his knowledge of Italian, was utterly charming in return.

'Fifteen minutes,' he said, turning around to her. 'And she's recommended a restaurant in the nearest village. Nothing fancy, of course. Simple home-cooked fare, and she ought to know. Her husband runs it.' He grinned and she felt weakly, numbingly conscious of him.

'Now that you've done your duty and accompanied me over, there's really no need for you to remain, you know.'

'Charming to the very last,' he said coolly, and Jessica flushed in acknowledgement of the home truth. She didn't trust herself to be open and friendly with him, though. In some part of her mind she felt that the only way to fight her attraction towards him was to outstretch both hands and keep him very firmly at a distance.

'I'm only saying what's on my mind.'

'For which I'm deeply grateful.' He didn't look deeply grateful. He looked deeply turned off, and she had an insane desire to make excuses for her abruptness even though logic told her that she had nothing to apologise about.

When it comes to love, she thought, any tactic in the world is acceptable, and that includes sidestepping courtesy.

The thought, which flashed into her mind so quickly that she barely had time to capture it, made her freeze in sudden, breathless awareness.

What did love have to do with anything? She felt faint as all the pieces of the puzzle began to fall neatly into place. Her reaction to him whenever he was around, the way he occupied her thoughts when he wasn't, the way all her perspectives on herself and on her life had been changing ever since he'd appeared on the scene, the way his relationship with his son mattered to her. The thousand and one inconsistencies which she had blithely put down to unwanted sexual attraction.

Sexual attraction was something she could handle, however difficult a beast it was for her. It was something she had not experienced for a lifetime, but she could at least acknowledge that she had finally fallen victim to it and that it was not incurable.

Love, on the other hand, was a horse of a completely different colour.

She closed her eyes and felt as though she was suffocating under the impact of the realisation.

How on earth could this *thing*, this unwelcome emotion, creep up on her like this? It was hardly as though she was on the market, looking for romance. Just the opposite. She was terrified at the thought of it.

'Are you all right?' Anthony asked, which made her jump because her thoughts had been miles away.

She made a big effort to gather herself together and present him with a smile that wasn't a reflection of her chaotic mind.

'Fine. Why shouldn't I be?' Had he seen anything on her face? Had he somehow short-circuited her brain and read what she had been thinking? She desperately hoped not. Loving him was bad enough, but for him to know would somehow be worse.

He was staring at her, his eyes probing. When, she wondered, had sexual interest turned into that deeper, more hungry emotion? She thought of Fiona, poor Fiona. How many hearts had he unwittingly broken along the way? Ten? A hundred? A thousand? The very fact that he probably didn't realise the devastating effect he could have on women made him far more lethal than any out-and-out cad.

She met his stare blandly and smiled back.

'I don't recall passing through too many little villages on the way here,' she said, snatching at the least perilous topic of conversation she could think of. 'Where exactly is this restaurant?'

He continued to look at her steadily and silently for a few seconds more, then he half nodded, as though mentally agreeing to let the matter of her sudden change of colour drop.

'To the north of this place. We approached from the south. From what Caterina said...'

'Caterina...?'

'The Moustache. From what she said, this particular village is positively throbbing with activity, though I'm inclined to take that with a pinch of salt, considering the vested interest she has in sending us there.'

'You mean her connection to this restaurant...?' More than ever it was imperative to keep her voice light and the conversation innocuous. He was a master at reading invisible signals and body language. He could write a book on the subject.

'And various other establishments. I gather she comes from a rather sprawling family.'

Jessica smiled politely and thought of hundreds of lookalikes with moustaches and dark hair running all the businesses in the town. Spooky.

'Let's hope we don't get the same taxi driver who brought us here,' she said in a friendly enough voice, but not meeting his eyes. 'He drove so slowly we'd be lucky if we made it there for breakfast tomorrow.'

Anthony laughed, and when the taxi finally arrived he harked back to what she had said, making an appropriately amusing remark, but as soon as they were on their way he turned to face her, stretching his arm along the back of the seat so that his fingers could easily brush the nape of her neck.

'What's bugging you?' he asked her averted profile. 'Did I inadvertently overstep the off-limits sign?'

Jessica glanced quickly at him, unamused. 'Why do you find it funny that I'm a private person?'

'Did you hear me laughing?'

'I didn't need to. I could hear the amusement in your voice. I can't help the way that I am.'

'And perish the thought that I might ever want to change you,' he said in a low voice which was neither serious nor jovial but somewhere disconcertingly in between.

'I suppose,' Jessica volunteered, simply because she wanted to edge away from the topic, 'I feel a little silly at having rushed all the way out here like a protective mother hen, only to find Lucy well and fine and in control.' A little truth, she thought, went a long way to successfully camouflaging the bigger, more worrying truth underneath.

True, she did feel a little stupid over her decision to jump on the first plane and confront her daughter, but on the whole she was glad that she had done so. Glad that she had not remained in England, stewing and imagining the worst. This little episode, for what it was worth, had set her mind at rest, and had probably paved the way for a great deal more trust in what her daughter did.

However, Anthony wasn't to know that that wasn't her main, consuming worry.

'I've spent so long investing my life in Luce that it's been a little difficult admitting to myself that it's time to let go.'

'Understandable.'

'So there—my thoughts all laid out on the table.'

'And very nicely arranged as well.' Which made her glance sharply at him, but his expression was mild enough, and she decided that she was just imagining the scepticism in his voice.

'What did you do with Mark when Lucy and I vanished?' she asked.

The taxi was making great headway. No dawdling on the road. This guy intended to make it to the village in record time, and Jessica couldn't have thanked him enough. The sooner he got there, the sooner they ate, and the sooner they left.

'Ah.' He removed his arm and loosely linked his fingers together.

'What kind of answer is ''ah''?' Freed from the discomfort of having her own motives queried, Jessica relaxed back in the seat and gave him her very fullest attention. Out of the corner of her eye she could see the countryside parting to accommodate the village, which was picturesque without trying. It was obvious that the place was no tourist stopover, and consequently there were no concessions to tourism. No fancy boutiques, no souvenir shops, no fast-food places. There were quite a few people around, though admittedly not many of them appeared to be doing anything of pressing urgency. In fact, most were enjoying the sun and doing absolutely nothing—small groups of weathered men and women, chatting about who knew what.

'He seemed unreasonably pleased that I was taking an interest in what he was doing.' He looked down, and Jessica noticed, with great tenderness, how his dark eyelashes hid the expression in his eyes. 'For which,' he said, looking up and catching her by surprise so that she resumed her guarded, polite interest, 'I have you to thank.'

'I realise that it was none of my business—'

'I wasn't being sarcastic,' he interrupted, and a dull flush crept through his face. 'Anyway, he showed me some of his work. It's not what I can really understand, but it's impressive. In its own way, of course.'

'Of course.' She smiled. The first smile of genuine warmth since she had seen him for the first time after all those weeks of silence.

'I'm rather more comfortable with paintings that depict things that are recognisable, but I'm willing to admit that Mark's work has a certain flair...'

The taxi slowed in front of a restaurant which was doing a good job of trying to resemble a café, and Anthony edged away from the conversation with an expression of relief. She felt another wave of quite unnecessary tenderness sweep over her at this show of masculine vulnerability.

She would have to watch herself, she knew. Now that she had admitted to herself what she felt for this man, it seemed as though her emotions were sabotaging her at every turn.

Inside, the restaurant was busy and basic, and the proprietor flamboyantly friendly.

'Perhaps we should have brought Lucy along here,' Anthony whispered in her ear as they were led towards their table. 'She might live to eat her words that the cafeteria at the campus wasn't quite up to my standards.'

'Lucy doesn't mean...'

'I know.' He shot her a look of perfect comprehension. 'She wants to shock.'

'She doesn't yet realise that maturity somehow makes it much harder to be shocked by anything.'

'Maturity and an ability to read the newspapers.'

They ordered from a limited menu, and then he leaned back and looked at her broodingly.

'I have a proposition to put to you,' he said finally.

'What?' She felt her stomach clench suddenly, and was keenly aware of how every small variation in the conversation, every tiny step into the unknown, could send her into a paroxysm of nerves.

'Why don't you take a few days off work and let me show you around Italy?'

'You must be joking.' She could tell from the look on his face that he wasn't, though. He meant every word of what he was saying.

'I'm being perfectly serious. How long is it since you had a break? Somewhere abroad?'

Jessica didn't know quite what was going on, but every instinct in her body was telling her that she should be careful. The waiter brought them their plates of spit-barbecued chicken, pulses, bread and potatoes, along with a carafe of white wine, and she gave the food and drink a great deal of attention.

'Well?' He began eating, although his attention wasn't on his food. It was focused entirely on her. He took a mouthful of wine and continued to search her face over the rim of the glass.

'Don't be ridiculous.' Jessica reached for her wine-glass but found that her hand was trembling, so she quickly withdrew it and speared some food with her fork instead.

'Why am I being ridiculous?' No nerves there, she noticed. He plunged into his food with enthusiasm.

'Because we hardly know one another...'

'I'd say we know each other rather well...'

'We've been through all this, Anthony. I thought I made it clear—I'm not interested in—'

'I know what you're not interested in,' he cut in. 'You might like to know that I'm not interested in a one-night-stand relationship with you either. Or a one-month stand, for that matter.'

Jessica couldn't help it. She felt her heart roll over inside her, and she had the dizzy sensation of being poised on the edge of a precipice. What was he saying? That he wanted a committed relationship with her? She could read nothing from his expression, but her mind somersaulted towards those meanings between the lines. Was he talking about love? Was it possible that he felt the same way that she did?

'We both have job commitments,' she said weakly, gamely trying not to surrender to something she desperately wanted to hear.

'I run the show. My commitments are ones that I lay down for myself. And I'm sure that your boss would oblige. After all, it's not as though you've only been there for a few months.'

'I know, but…'

'But what?' He closed his knife and fork and regarded her seriously.

'I haven't come prepared…' She wasn't refusing him. She knew that. She could hear the indecision in her voice, the wavering of someone who hoped to be persuaded.

'We can sort that out.'

'I don't understand why you're throwing this proposal at me,' she said finally. *Because you love me?* It was what she wanted to hear. She yearned for the declaration.

'Because I like you,' Anthony said calmly, 'I need a

rest, and I suspect you do as well. We're here; it seems almost too good an opportunity to pass up. What better way to see a bit of Italy than with a friend?'

CHAPTER TEN

W ᴇ ɴ had the term 'friend' ever had a more crushingly disappointing ring? His words floated over her head and then poured over her like a bucket of ice water, pulling her up short and banishing any cosy little assumptions she might have been forming.

Jessica looked at him, dry-mouthed and clear-eyed. On every level Anthony Newman was a man way out of her league, whatever minor indiscretions might have taken place between them in the past. A combination of fate and coincidence had thrown them together. Under normal circumstances they would never have met, not in a hundred years, and even if they had they would have met as the strangers that they were. Two people from two different worlds who only had the minimum in common.

Fiona might not quite have been his cup of tea, but she belonged to that particular genre of woman who was. He was wealthy, powerful, charismatic. Since when did his type fall in love with humble secretaries? If she'd worked in his office, he would probably have walked past her desk every day without noticing her.

Their one act of lovemaking had not, she saw now, been the result of any interested pursuit on his part. More a situation that had arisen through an extraordinary combination of circumstances. The very same way that people could sometimes meet on holiday, be violently attracted to someone to whom they normally wouldn't have given a second glance had they been in their own surroundings.

It made her feel almost worse to know that he liked her. He *liked* her. The way someone liked their kid sister's best friend. No wonder he saw nothing unreasonable about his proposal. He was right—a week in Italy, with a friend, would be a very pleasant way of passing the time and de-stressing. And he probably felt that she needed it. Another charitable gesture. The man was full of them. Except charity from him was the one thing she didn't need.

'That's a very kind suggestion,' Jessica told him, leaning back in her chair so that the waiter could clear the table, and then shaking her head at the offer of dessert. Right now she just wanted to get back to the campus, find whatever room had been reserved for her, climb into bed, and hide her head under a pillow.

'Kindness had nothing to do with it.' His eyes took on a flinty look. 'I'm not in the business of playing Father Christmas and dispensing favours.'

'Well,' Jessica said vaguely, 'whatever…'

'No, *not* "whatever".' He leaned forward, resting his elbows on the table, linking his fingers together, and although the table separated them she still had to fight the urge to cringe back, simply to escape the overpowering impact of his personality.

'It's that damn pig-headed pride of yours, isn't it?' His voice was low and cold and jabbed into her like a knife, prodding her into a reaction she didn't want to give.

'Thank you very much for that. Any more compliments from where that one came from?'

'Oh, give me a minute; I could think of dozens.' He leaned back in the chair and surveyed her with that unwavering, cold look that made her feel like a very small, very helpless animal cornered by something altogether bigger and more terrifying.

'Come on, let's head back to the campus, and on the way you can tell me in detail exactly why you find my proposition so unacceptable.' He stood up and Jessica hurriedly followed suit. When she offered to settle half the bill he glared at her, which didn't stop her from defiantly leaving a tip on the table.

'I really can't spare the time for days off from work,' Jessica began, when they finally managed to locate a taxi driver and persuade him that driving them to the campus was a better deal than snoozing under a tree in the square. 'I've been falling behind recently, and I can't afford to let my standards begin to slip. Apart from anything else, I've worked there for a long time, and I wouldn't like them to feel that I'm losing my touch.' She hated herself for lying, but then it was so much easier than launching into the truth.

'I'm touched by your zealous attitude towards your job,' he told her sarcastically. 'But you'll have to forgive me if I don't quite believe you.'

'Fine.' Jessica stared out of the window, conscious that her body language was saying a great deal about her frame of mind. Poised, stiff-backed, on the edge of the seat, her fists balled. 'I forgive you.'

'Dammit, Jessica, look at me.'

Jessica threw him a glance. 'Or else what?'

'Or else I'll make this a very interesting ride for our taxi driver up front.'

Since the taxi driver already appeared to be very interested in what was going on in the back seat of his car, Jessica turned and faced Anthony.

'By doing what?' she enquired politely. 'Pinning me

to the seat of the car until you get another answer out of me?'

'If that's what it takes.'

They stared at one another in silence. Over and above the sound of the car trudging along, Jessica could hear the blood rushing through her, the unsteady beat of her heart. When she swallowed, she could even hear the motion of her throat.

'Why? Why does it matter one way or another? Can't your pride suffer a little knock because I've turned your offer down?'

'This isn't a question of pride.' He turned away from her in apparent frustration, and she resumed her mindless gazing at the scenery. Between them the air hung heavy with unspoken words, words which she tried to interpret, but couldn't. She just knew that her nerves were jangling, and there wasn't a part of her that didn't want out of the taxi and away from the man sitting next to her. How could fate pull such a low trick on her? All these years she'd been so careful with her emotions, only to find that in the end it amounted to nothing. Love still came along and tripped her up when she was least expecting it.

Also, he hadn't answered her question, and that was niggling away at her, even though the greater part of her didn't want it answered because she knew what he would say. That he liked her, that he found her pleasant, personable company. All those adjectives that basically meant the opposite of sexy, the opposite of attractive.

The taxi deposited them at the campus, and Jessica avoided the taxi driver's eyes. They were too blatantly curious for her liking. He couldn't have understood a word they had been saying, she thought, yet he looked as though he had caught on to the situation without too much difficulty and was intrigued.

'If you don't mind, I think I'll head up to my room now and wait for Luce.' She didn't give him time to answer. She collected the keys from Reception and somehow found her way to a spacious enough two-bedroom dormitory which, since it was empty of clothing, she assumed she would not be sharing with anyone. The place was not a hotel and she knew well enough that they could easily have placed her in a shared room, which was the last thing she wanted. Company she could do without.

She now opened the holdall she had retrieved from Lucy's room *en route*, and extracted some fresh clothes from it. Of course, the shower was shared, but the trip into the village had made her hot and sweaty, and traipsing along the corridor with only a towel for cover was a small price to pay for the feel of cool water splashing over her.

Besides, the place was more or less empty. Obviously this was peak time for classes. No doubt as evening approached the students would start returning. With a sudden, disorientating flash of insight, she realised what a good thing it was that her daughter had come to this place, had seen for herself the camaraderie and fun of this kind of university life. It would encourage her not to allow her chance of a university education to be stillborn.

She stood outside the bedroom door, not wet but still damp from the shower, and listened to the silence, enjoying the feel of it, then she pushed open the bedroom door, stepped inside, and saw him immediately, sitting upright on the one and only chair in the room.

Her immediate thought was to run away. Except, with

just a towel around her, it occurred to her that she would hardly get very far. At least, not without dying of embarrassment on the way. But she didn't know what to do, so she hovered by the doorway, then finally pushed it shut behind her and said, leaning against it, 'What are you doing in my room?'

'Correction, *our* room.' He made no move towards her, but his eyes were enough to throw her into a state of impotent panic.

'This is my room. I got the key from the receptionist…'

'Apparently the place is packed. Summer camp here is filled to capacity. In fact, we only got this room thanks to some clever rearranging of the girls who were in it.'

Jessica looked at him with mounting dismay.

'Well, you'll have to try and fix something else up.'

'Why? There are two beds, aren't there?'

'I refuse to share a room with you.'

'Because you think that I might jump on you? Which is the same reason that you refused my offer of a holiday?'

'No!'

'Then what's the problem?'

'The problem is…that I want some privacy…'

'You can't run away from me, Jessica.' He stood up and lazily strolled towards her, hands in pockets, eyes firmly fixed on her face. He mesmerised her. She found that she couldn't move, as though she'd been paralysed by a stun gun and could now only watch the impending threat approach with her heart in her mouth and absolutely no co-operation from her limbs.

'I'm not doing anything of the sort…' She heard the panic in her voice, but was incapable of doing anything about it. In desperation, she clutched the towel around her a little tighter.

'I won't let you go.'

She had drawn the curtains before she'd left, and the light filtering through gave the room a mellow golden hue.

'What do you mean?' she whispered.

He didn't answer immediately. Instead, he took her by the arms, rubbing his thumbs against the softness of her flesh, a gesture which Jessica tried very hard not to notice.

'What do you think I mean?'

'I'm not on the lookout for friends,' she told him in confusion. 'I…'

'Nor am I.'

'But…you said…'

'I know what I said. I had my reasons.'

Now she was beginning to feel weak, but she couldn't sit down. The short distance between the door and the chair would be her undoing. So she remained stock-still.

'What reason? I need to sit down. No, I need to get dressed.'

He stepped aside and she waited for him to leave, but he didn't, and rather than remain standing in a state of total indecision and confusion she made her way to the chair and sat down. A bit of a mistake as it turned out, since the towel now rode up, revealing so much of her thighs that she was forced into the embarrassing dilemma of keeping it over her breasts whilst tugging it down, so that she maintained some semblance of decorum.

And, worse, he followed her languidly to where she was sitting and squatted by the chair. She could feel her skin prickle from his proximity, and the fine hairs on her legs stood on end, as though responding to electricity in his body.

'Why do you think I came over here to Italy?' he asked in a low, serious voice. 'This is a ridiculously furnished room,' he continued. 'There aren't sufficient chairs. In a minute my legs are going to go into severe cramp.'

'Students probably just flop around on beds,' Jessica replied in a dazed voice.

'So, shall we?'

'No!'

'I thought you might say that. At least do me the favour of sitting on the ground so that we're on the same level. What I have to say to you is difficult enough without the distraction of paralysis from the waist down.'

Jessica wriggled her way to the ground and sat with her legs sticking out straight in front of her, and regarded him solemnly as he sat next to her.

'Why do you think I came to Italy with you?' he repeated.

'Because you felt responsible... Maybe you thought that Mark had somehow coerced Lucy...'

'Not at all.' He gave her a small, sardonic smile. 'I doubt if Lucy could be coerced into anything. She strikes me as the sort of girl who's as stubborn as they come and will do precisely as she sees fit. Like her bewitching mother.'

Jessica didn't bother to analyse this description of her daughter. Her brain focused on the word 'bewitching' and held onto it, savouring it the way a man dying of thirst savours the first sip of water.

'I came because I had to,' he said bluntly. 'I came because the last few weeks without you have been hell, and this opportunity came along and fell into my lap and I had to take advantage of it.'

Jessica's mouth refused point-blank to make any response to this statement.

'Frankly, if it hadn't come up, I would have contacted you anyway. I would have used any excuse in the book, done anything to get back into your life.'

How can someone get back to a place they never left? she wanted to ask. But she didn't dare phrase the question. She had misread signals in the past, and optimism, however alluring, was not an emotion she was about to give in to now.

'I've never felt this way about anyone in my life before,' he told her, and even without looking at him she could hear from the unsteady tenor of his voice that the admission did not come easily.

'Felt what way?' she asked in a whisper.

'Felt involved. Felt as though what happened in your life was as important as what happened in my own. Felt as though you were somehow as much a part of me as the organs in my body.'

Jessica inclined her body slightly so that she was facing him now, her eyes wide with hope and an insatiable desire to hear more.

'You have this effect on me,' he told her with a short, bewildered laugh.

'It's mutual,' she said in a low voice. Had she said too much? Was she misreading signals again? It didn't seem so—at least not judging from the expression on his face.

'I'm not talking about friendship.'

'No.'

'I want more than friendship, Jessica, I want...' He hesitated, as though searching around for the right words. 'I want everything. I want you to need me, to want me, to find life unliveable without me. I want you to feel all the things for me that I feel for you.'

Years of caution finally dropped off her shoulders. The past, which she had carried around with her like an invisible burden, no longer mattered. All that mattered was this man sitting right here on the ground next to her; he was the present and the future. He eclipsed all those things that had turned her into the wary, distrusting person she had been for such a long time. He liberated her, and it was a heady, wonderful feeling.

She gave him a tremulous smile.

'I never imagined...' she said. Her hand moved of its own volition, reaching out to stroke the side of his face, and he took it in his hands and turned it over, palm upwards, smothering it with hungry little kisses.

'I'm in love with you, Jessica.' He raised his eyes to look at her. 'I've laughed at the possibility, denied it vigorously, told myself that it was just a passing ailment, like swine fever, but it's no good. I'm hopelessly in love with you, and I intend to pursue you until you feel exactly the same way about me. And I'll warn you from now that I'll resort to any tactics that I can.'

'Okay.' She gave a low, amazed laugh. 'That sounds fine, but you might find that there's no need.' She was as unused to emotional declarations as he apparently was, but there was no need for her to declare anything. It was there in her eyes, and he bent his head towards her. She felt the touch of his mouth against hers and was instantly lost.

'God knows,' he groaned, 'you've turned my life on its head. Since you came along, you've forced me to put my life into perspective...'

'How terrible!' She gave a low chuckle and eased her

body back, pulling him towards her. The towel, which she had been holding in a precarious grip only minutes before, unravelled around her, and she watched with satisfaction as his eyes roamed hungrily over her nudity.

'It serves you right,' she told him, 'because you've had the same effect on me. Like being caught up in a cyclone on an otherwise bright and sunny day.'

He laughed and kissed her neck as she blindly unfastened the buttons of his shirt and eased her hands against his chest, loving the strong, hard feel of his muscle against them. Her breasts, arching upwards, yearned for the sensation of his mouth circling them, and, as though reading her thoughts, he trailed his lips along her collarbone, finding his way to one nipple and sucking it deeply into his mouth, making her arch her body yet more so that she pressed hard against him. Whilst his hand sought the dampness between her legs that reflected her mounting passion, she rolled her other nipple in between her fingers, massaging her breast until his mouth replaced her hand.

He only paused in his lovemaking to remove his clothes, and this she watched with undisguised pleasure, delighting in the lines of his body.

Somewhere in the world there were better bodies, she supposed, but for the life of her it was a concept that she couldn't quite take on board. He was perfection— body and mind in perfect harmony. Or was she being biased?

She closed her eyes and breathed hotly as he trailed his tongue along the insides of her thighs, kneading them at the same time with his hands, then his probing tongue found her most intimate place, and she groaned with abandonment and pleasure as he tasted her. A slow, deliberate exploration. She could feel the tip of his tongue flicking, arousing, sending her into a frenzy of desire, then his mouth drawing the wetness out of her into him.

His hands found her breasts once again, and she was still throbbing between her legs as he held both breasts in his hands, pushing them up so that her engorged nipples were like two ripe, plump fruits waiting to be sampled.

'You're beautiful,' he said, almost talking to himself, she felt, rather than her.

He nibbled her nipples, licked and teased them with his tongue and his teeth until she was squirming against him, and she felt his hardness against her and reached down to grip him, slowly massaging until the only sounds in the room were their breathing and the erotic movements of body against body.

When he finally thrust into her, self-control was out of the question. They had gone too far to hold back. Jessica felt the electrifying sensation of climax, then the pleasurable ripples of its aftermath coursing through her veins, leaving her drowsy and satiated.

'So,' he said, breaking the silence and cupping her face in his hands, 'what do you say now about a week or two touring Italy? Do you think that your conscience might allow you the time off work?'

'I think it might well,' Jessica replied contentedly. This must be how the cat felt when it got its bowl of cream, lapped it all up, and knew that there was a great deal more whence it had come.

'And what about those teenage appendages of ours? What do you think their reaction will be when we break the news to them?'

'Oh, I think Lucy will be fine. She knows that I need a holiday.'

'Actually, I wasn't talking about the holiday.' He

kissed the tip of her nose and smiled. 'I was more re-
ferring to the ring I intend to put on your finger just as
soon as I can.'

'Marriage is a big step…perhaps we ought to test the
water first…'

'Perhaps not.'

They looked at one another and Jessica laughed, and
then sighed with pure contentment.

'You can be so persuasive. Okay, then. Perhaps not…'

4 FREE

books and a surprise gift!

We would like to take this opportunity to thank you for reading this Mills & Boon® book by offering you the chance to take FOUR more specially selected titles from the Presents™ series absolutely FREE! We're also making this offer to introduce you to the benefits of the Reader Service™—

- ★ FREE home delivery
- ★ FREE gifts and competitions
- ★ FREE monthly newsletter
- ★ Books available before they're in the shops
- ★ Exclusive Reader Service discounts

Accepting these FREE books and gift places you under no obligation to buy, you may cancel at any time, even after receiving your free shipment. Simply complete your details below and return the entire page to the address below. *You don't even need a stamp!*

YES! Please send me 4 free Presents books and a surprise gift. I understand that unless you hear from me, I will receive 6 superb new titles every month for just £2.30 each, postage and packing free. I am under no obligation to purchase any books and may cancel my subscription at any time. The free books and gift will be mine to keep in any case.

P8XE

Ms/Mrs/Miss/Mr ....Initials ....
BLOCK CAPITALS PLEASE

Surname ....

Address ....

....

....Postcode...................................

Send this whole page to:
THE READER SERVICE, FREEPOST, CROYDON, CR9 3WZ
(Eire readers please send coupon to: P.O. BOX 4546, DUBLIN 24.)

Offer not valid to current Reader Service subscribers to this series. We reserve the right to refuse an application and applicants must be aged 18 years or over. Only one application per household. Terms and prices subject to change without notice. Offer expires 30th September 1998. You may be mailed with offers from other reputable companies as a result of this application. If you would prefer not to receive such offers, please tick box. ☐
Mills & Boon® Presents™ is a registered trademark of Harlequin Mills & Boon Ltd.

MILLS & BOON®

Next Month's Romances

$\heartsuit$

Each month you can choose from a wide variety of romance novels from Mills & Boon®. Below are the new titles to look out for next month from the Presents™ and Enchanted™ series.

Presents™

SINFUL PLEASURES	Anne Mather
THE RELUCTANT HUSBAND	Lynne Graham
THE NANNY AFFAIR	Robyn Donald
RUNAWAY FIANCÉE	Sally Wentworth
THE BRIDE'S SECRET	Helen Brooks
TEMPORARY PARENTS	Sara Wood
CONTRACT WIFE	Kay Thorpe
RED-HOT LOVER	Sarah Holland

Enchanted™

AN IDEAL WIFE	Betty Neels
DASH TO THE ALTAR	Ruth Jean Dale
JUST ANOTHER MIRACLE!	Caroline Anderson
ELOPING WITH EMMY	Liz Fielding
THE WEDDING TRAP	Eva Rutland
LAST CHANCE MARRIAGE	Rosemary Gibson
MAX'S PROPOSAL	Jane Donnelly
LONE STAR LOVIN'	Debbie Macomber

On sale from 6th April 1998

H1 9803

Available at most branches of
WH Smith, John Menzies, Martins, Tesco,
Asda, Volume One, Sainsbury and Safeway

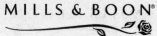

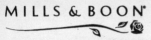

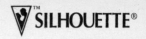

We have teamed up with Flying Flowers, the UK's premier 'flowers by post' company, to offer you £5 off a choice of their two most popular bouquets the 18 mix (CAS) of 10 multihead and 8 luxury bloom Carnations and the 25 mix (CFG) of 15 luxury bloom Carnations, 10 Freesias and Gypsophila. All bouquets contain fresh flowers 'in bud', added greenery, bouquet wrap, flower food, care instructions, and personal message card. They are boxed, gift wrapped and sent by 1st class post.

To redeem £5 off a Flying Flowers bouquet, simply complete the application form below and send it with your cheque or postal order to; **HMB Flying Flowers Offer, The Jersey Flower Centre, Jersey JE1 5FF.**

SPECIAL OFFER £5 OFF

FLYING FLOWERS

Beautiful fresh flowers, sent by 1st class post to any UK and Eire address.

ORDER FORM (Block capitals please) Valid for delivery anytime until 30th November 1998 MAB/0298/A

Title .... Initials .... Surname ....

Address ....

.... Postcode ....

Signature .... Are you a Reader Service Subscriber **YES/NO**

Bouquet(s) **18 CAS** (Usual Price £14.99) **£9.99** ☐   **25 CFG** (Usual Price £19.99) **£14.99** ☐

I enclose a cheque/postal order payable to Flying Flowers for £ .... or payment by

VISA/MASTERCARD ☐☐☐☐☐☐☐☐☐☐☐☐☐☐☐☐ Expiry Date .... / .... /..........

PLEASE SEND MY BOUQUET TO ARRIVE BY .... / .... / ....

TO Title .... Initials .... Surname ....

Address ....

.... Postcode ....

Message (Max 10 Words) ....

Please allow a minimum of four working days between receipt of order and 'required by date' for delivery.

You may be mailed with offers from other reputable companies as a result of this application. Please tick box if you would prefer not to receive such offers. ☐

Terms and Conditions Although dispatched by 1st class post to arrive by the required date the exact day of delivery cannot be guaranteed. Valid for delivery anytime until 30th November 1998. Maximum of 5 redemptions per household, photocopies of the voucher will be accepted.